HARMONUS LEGACY

HARMONUS LEGACY
THE FIRST WAR

JACK HARMON

authorHOUSE

AuthorHouse™
1663 Liberty Drive
Bloomington, IN 47403
www.authorhouse.com
Phone: 1 (800) 839-8640

© 2015 Jacob Harmon. All rights reserved.

No part of this book may be reproduced, stored in a retrieval system, or transmitted by any means without the written permission of the author.

Published by AuthorHouse   08/19/2015

ISBN: 978-1-5049-3239-4 (sc)
ISBN: 978-1-5049-3240-0 (hc)
ISBN: 978-1-5049-3238-7 (e)

Library of Congress Control Number: 2015913476

Print information available on the last page.

Any people depicted in stock imagery provided by Thinkstock are models, and such images are being used for illustrative purposes only.
Certain stock imagery © Thinkstock.

This book is printed on acid-free paper.

Because of the dynamic nature of the Internet, any web addresses or links contained in this book may have changed since publication and may no longer be valid. The views expressed in this work are solely those of the author and do not necessarily reflect the views of the publisher, and the publisher hereby disclaims any responsibility for them.

To Ross,

Thank you for being a good fan and a great friend.

Please reach out if I can help you with anything.

"You define yourself by the legacy you leave behind."

— Harmon

Prologue

This is a story about a world that lives off of an essence called *teva*. Teva is a magic that creates and sustains life. No being dies of age and no natural resources are depleted as long as the teva is allowed to sustain them. The aggelos were the first to be created in this world and are the lords of the land. They stood two meters tall with silken, silver hair and fair skin. Before time was recorded, there were eighteen aggelos lords. They could influence all aspects of teva in the smallest way, but each one could only control a very specific aspect of teva. Of all the aggelos, Airandrius is the oldest and strongest, making him *lekavot* (or king). He rules the land of Nivine with absolute authority. With the presence of an aggelos in the land, the sun would never stop shining; thus instead of looking at the sun to count the days, people looked at the moon.

Chapter 1: Peace

Harmonus had a headache from concentrating. Just two days prior he had sent an explosion of energy from his staff toward a target he had set up and turned the target into ash. He thought back on how he did it. He tried to make the hair on the back of his neck stand like it did before. He thought of the thunderous sound the flash made. Two days had passed since he sent that flash from his staff, and for two days he hadn't moved. He closed his eyes with his staff still aimed at the boulder. He felt the teva throughout the land. He could feel it nourishing the plants and even the very air. Harmonus was the lord of hope and light, but unlike the other aggelos, Harmonus had a unique ability to siphon the teva out of the land and even out of other people. This ability was dangerous, and Harmonus had to learn at a very young age to control it so he wouldn't kill all those around him. He thought about letting his ability come out and drawing in the teva from the land but then quickly dismissed the idea. An aggelos had a very high amount of teva compared to the newly born men. He had also summoned the flash of light before; he didn't need any more teva. He just needed to control his abilities. Harmonus couldn't help but smile. He thought back on his uncle Azekiel training him on how to use his abilities.

"May we leave now? Mother will be looking for us." Harmonus looked down at his little brother. He was just a few years old. His silver hair was just long enough to reach his blue eyes. It reminded Harmonus of how he had looked so many ages before.

"I'm sure mother can find us if she wishes, Korvinus. Where is Airia?"

"I'm here, Harmonus." Harmonus looked around the plain until he saw a large brown tree with dark green leaves. He could sense Airia was up in the tree. She stepped out on a thin branch, and he could see her long, silver hair waving in the wind. Unlike Korvinus and himself, Airia had their mother's face. Most men find it hard to tell the difference between the aggelos, and most aggelos find it hard to tell the difference between Airia and her mother, Ameela. Airia jumped down from the branch with a feline elegance. "Still trying to make that flash like you did earlier." She said it more like a statement than a question but Harmonus decided to answer her anyway.

"I keep thinking of the moment I let the light loose, trying to figure out how I felt during the time or what I did so I can do it again."

Airia tilted her head to the left a little, pondering. "I remember when Uncle Azekiel was training me on my healing abilities, he told me that some abilities require us to take teva from others or from the land because we are not lords of that particular aspect of teva. Then he said if you are using a teva that you are the lord over, then you must find it within yourself, whether it be through emotions or concentration."

Harmonus thought about what his younger sister said. Airia came to this land just before man, yet she seemed like she had been here just as long as Harmonus. He tried it again, this time with emotion. He let his staff down, and then shot it out in front of him. Nothing. Harmonus felt his anger rising. His right arm started to glow with light blue lines running up his arm from the staff. The hair on his arm started to rise. He felt the power rising from his back to his arm into his staff. Then he released it. At first there was a crackle, and then a thunder echoed through the air. Airia and Korvinus stared with wide eyes as their older brother released an endless light from the tip of his staff. Their silky hair now stood on end from the electricity. The ground melted under the bolt of light. When Harmonus stopped, he looked at his younger siblings. They were covering their ears but staring in wonder at the rock he had just melted.

"I see you've been practicing." Harmonus jumped. He hadn't sensed anyone coming up behind him. He turned around and saw a massive aggelos who stood a little over two meters tall and had long silver hair down to his upper back and white stubble on his face. He was wearing a white robe with a white half-cape on his left shoulder, signifying his position as a councilman among the aggelos.

"Azekiel, you startled me. What brings my uncle down from the mountains?"

"Your mother and father were looking for you. They wondered if you were training with me again. I had actually been looking for you for a while when I heard the thunder." His voice was husky and bold.

"Me?" They were never concerned of Harmonus's whereabouts. If anything, Ameela would wonder where Airia or Korvinus was. "Did they mention why?"

"Neither one told me anything, but it didn't seem urgent. I don't think it's something to fret over. When did you learn to do that?" Azekiel pointed at the melted rock.

"I was trying to teach Korvinus how to command teva by lifting and sending rocks at the target." Harmonus pointed over at the dummy they had set up some days before. "It seems I don't have the patience that you do. I became agitated and destroyed it by accident." Azekiel gave a look of approval and nodded. Of all the aggelos lords, Azekiel knew the most about teva, followed closely by Abbadon. But Harmonus never liked Abbadon, even though many think that he and Abbadon are very closely related when it comes to their abilities. Harmonus sucked the teva out of his surroundings naturally, an ability that Abbadon obsessively practiced. Harmonus had to learn to block this ability so he wouldn't harm or possibly kill anyone, while Abbadon had to train for years to be able to do it. This ability didn't sit well with the other lords, so Azekiel took Harmonus his wing to teach him how to get a better control of his abilities. Abbadon, meanwhile, was commanded never to use the ability again. Harmonus didn't mind Azekiel. In fact he rather enjoyed being around Azekiel and Kav'wai, Azekiel's son and Harmonus's best friend.

"Come. It's time we got back to Nicile." Nicile was the capital of Nivine, land of the aggelos. Harmonus let go of his staff, making it vanish as it always did. At birth, the aggelos are bound to a certain weapon called a *zeyak*. These weapons have their masters' names on them, and only their masters can summon and use them. But the zeyak was far more than a weapon. Azekiel realized that their zeyaks were what allowed them to study teva and truly master the arcane knowledge. The aggelos could also pour their teva into their zeyaks, which allowed them to center their teva on a certain thing.

"Uncle, when did you decide to study teva?" Harmonus was walking right behind Azekiel as he asked the question.

Azekiel looked over his right shoulder. "It was right after Abbadon's sire's died. I felt a fear rip at my heart. I wanted to learn everything I could about teva so I could find out how they died." Harmonus nodded and watched his uncle in front of him. Azekiel walked with an air of authority, as if nothing in the world could best him, but he didn't seem prideful. That gave Harmonus that extra sense of security, not that security mattered. Everyone followed the rules and the lekavot's commands, even the humans—everyone, that is, except his children, it seemed. At least, that's what everyone else seemed to think. Harmonus made sure his half-cape hooked over his left shoulder. Out of everything you wore, you had to make sure the half-cape looked presentable. It was a symbol that you were a lord and councilman of the aggelos, and Airandrius would be furious if his own son didn't respect his status symbol. Harmonus was the youngest of the lords, and many believed he only got on the council because his father was the lekavot. But that was just another thing Harmonus didn't care about. He didn't see the need for the council when Airandrius could always overrule their decisions. They never even got together unless Airandrius was present, so it wasn't as if they were handling things while he was away. There was never any reason for his father to be away; each city in Nivine was ruled by an aggelos family, and no man could match the power of an aggelos. On top of that, men who were loyal enough were made into guardsmen, who may fight a foul beast here and there but who for the most part just made sure to keep the peace. Why would the lekavot need to leave? He didn't feel the need to. He was always around to make sure his kingdom would continue to prosper.

"You seem to be deep in thought today," Azekiel said with a tender care that Airandrius never had. "What's on your mind?" Harmonus wanted to tell Azekiel the truth but decided not to. Azekiel had always been extremely loyal to his brother.

"I'm just curious as to why my father and mother would need me is all."

"I'm sure if it was something urgent they would be out here looking for you as well. How is the lovely Airia doing today?"

Airia hopped. "I am quite well, Uncle Azekiel. How are you?"

"I am doing well. I was able to spend some time with Kav'wai earlier, which always puts me in a good mood. What about the young Kor—" Azekiel turned around and stopped. "Where is Korvinus?"

Harmonus and Airia turned simultaneously. He was right behind them when they left, and they hadn't even gone far. Harmonus could still see the boulder he melted. Harmonus started yelling his brother's name, which seemed to carry in the wind across the plains. How could he simply wonder off? And why would he? Harmonus started to panic. He tried to think of anything that could harm a young aggelos.

"Relax, Harmonus," Azekiel said softly. "Remember how I taught you to feel everything around you." Harmonus took the hint and closed his eyes to feel the world around him. He could sense Airia and Azekiel right next to him. He pushed out further, feeling the teva in the air and ground. and then he felt it! Korvinus was in the tall grass to their left, his head lowered so no one could see him try to sneak up on his older siblings. Harmonus smiled and acted like he was still in a trance. Korvinus jumped out, and while he was in mid air, Harmonus charged and grabbed his younger brother. He moved so fast that he scared Korvinus.

Azekiel gave a hearty laugh. "You are getting even faster, Harmonus. Some day you may be able to move as fast as the light you command." Harmonus gave a smile to his younger brother. Korvinus tried to keep a pout on his face, but he couldn't hold it and started smiling as well. Harmonus let Korvinus down and continued to walk with his uncle. Harmonus couldn't help but look at the passing moon; the sun looked as if it had moved, but Harmonus figured he must have been pushing himself too hard. The sun wouldn't move in Nivine any more than the moon would stop.

When they finally reached Nicile, Harmonus couldn't help but marvel at the city. On the main road leading out of the front of the city, there are two huge statues of Airandrius holding his large, two-handed sword with the blade going into the ground. Waterfalls fell from the tops of houses into streams that flowed into one river that left the city to the east. All the buildings were about ten meters high and were made of white marble. There were no windows or doors to keep out the weather because the weather was always nice in a land ruled by an aggelos. The roads were made of a green glass, and water flowed beneath them. In the center of the city stood a palace that towered over the other buildings like a mountain. Harmonus had called that palace home for the past sixty years, ever since his father built the city with just his willpower.

They started walking to the front of the palace. The waterfalls in the city originated from the palace center. Harmonus always wondered where the water actually came from. When he asked his father, his father would simply say, "Sheer will." The water flowed down in a spiral around a spire in the center of the palace and into the separate pools or rivers that flowed through the palace.

Azekiel broke the silence. "Go see your mother, and then come see me when you get the chance. I want to see how you do with your breakthrough."

Harmonus nodded and turned to his younger siblings. "Let's go see what they want" he said. They followed obediently. Harmonus walked through the front entrance of the palace; the main entrance was flanked on each side with a guard. When they saw Harmonus approaching, they bowed their heads and the one on the right spoke up.

"Harmonus, how was your trip?"

Harmonus looked at their gray uniforms. Most guardsmen wore gray with swords sheathed on their left side. The royal guards, however, had some white silk sown into their gray and had helmets and spears instead of swords. Harmonus nodded his head in response to the question. "It was eventful. Have you seen the lekavot?"

"Apologies, I have not. Where are your guards?" The guard looked around to see if any guards were behind Harmonus.

"I don't need any guards, I assure you." The guard simply lowered his head in response. There was no need for a guard to follow Harmonus around. He was far more powerful than any human, and he didn't see the sense of putting lives in danger. If he couldn't protect himself, then there was no way a guard could protect him. Harmonus pressed on. The first room you came to when entering the palace was the throne room. There were four hallways from there. The first hallway on the left lead to the council chambers and dungeon. The second on the left lead to the treasury, the dining hall, and the stairs that lead to the upper-left wing of the palace. The first on the right lead to the royal rooms. The second on the right lead to the gardens and to a set of stairs that lead to the upper-right wing. Harmonus figured Ameela would be either in her room or in the gardens. Sure enough, she was in the gardens.

"You were looking for me, Mother?" Harmonus said.

Ameela turned around and gave a smile that would take away any worries in your heart. "Hello, Harmonus. It's good to see you. You two may leave; I just wanted to speak to your brother." Airia and Korvinus left as Ameela got up from her gardening and gave Harmonus a hug that seemed as if it was her last.

"Are you all right, Mother?"

"Yes. I've had a strange feeling lately, and I just wanted to make sure you were all right."

"Of course I'm all right. Why wouldn't I be?"

"Many changes are about to happen, Harmonus—changes that we will not be able to stop—and I simply wanted you to know that I love you."

"What are you going on about, Mother? Are you not feeling well?" Ameela was the mother of destiny and time. Many believed that she knew the very fate of the world. But premonition was not her only ability, for she could sense the life presence of every living being. She even felt the death of Abbadon's parents so far away though she didn't know why they died.

Ameela let her head drop to her chest. "You are going to become much more powerful, Harmonus. This power could destroy this precious world or save it. You are to be the only aggelos that walks this earth once the darkness is gone."

"What do you mean? What darkness?"

"Have you noticed the sun, Harmonus? How it has started moving across the sky?"

"I did see it earlier and thought it moved, but I wasn't sure. You mean to say the sun will set like the moon?"

Ameela shook her head. "Though the sun does set in other lands, that is not of what I speak. The light will be swallowed up in these lands. You will fight a terror that could destroy every living thing on this earth. If you hear anything I say, let it be this: do not give in to corruption, my son. Do not allow your power to destroy who you are."

Harmonus could only nod at what his mother was saying. He couldn't imagine the land being swallowed up in darkness.

Ameela placed her hand on her sons shoulder. "Sometimes I feel as if this foresight is more of a curse than a gift. Do not dwell on my words too much, my son, for there is nothing you can do to change the future. But enough of that. How is your training going?"

Harmonus had to hide his dreadful thoughts and come up with his answer. Ameela could enter your mind if you didn't keep your emotions in check, and Harmonus couldn't stand her in his mind. "It is going well. I was going to train with Azekiel in the after hour if I wasn't busy."

"Well you best not keep him waiting, then. I just wanted to make sure you were all right."

Harmonus left with a bow and quickly went to the highest level of the palace to escape his thoughts. The top level opened up into a large flat area with no walls or roof. Azekiel was already there on the far side, sitting at the edge of the platform and looking down into the city. When Harmonus saw Azekiel at the other end of the platform, he entered a battle trance. He thought about sneaking up on Azekiel but quickly dismissed the idea. Azekiel would sense him coming if he didn't already know he was there. His best bet would be to charge at him as fast as he could. Harmonus was the fastest of all the aggelos, even faster than Azekiel. But Azekiel was older and stronger as the lord of wisdom and knowledge; he knew how to influence teva to strengthen his already strong muscles and reactions.

Harmonus summoned his staff, and in a blink of an eye, he charged. Time seemed to slow when he moved this fast, and each time he charged, he seemed to go faster than the last time. Yet sure enough, Azekiel was ready for him. In the instant it took Harmonus to charge, Azekiel had already determined what Harmonus would do and simply brought his blade up behind him right in Harmonus's path. Harmonus stopped instantly but sent a shockwave of energy forward. Azekiel jumped high in the air, avoiding the shockwave, and then came down behind Harmonus with both of his curved blades out, ready to tear into Harmonus. Harmonus blocked the blades with his staff and then twisted his staff in an effort to make his opponent cross his arms. But Azekiel used the cross to slash horizontally, forcing Harmonus to push his staff out at Azekiel to avoid the slash. Harmonus's staff sent out a wave of energy that pushed Azekiel back, giving Harmonus some room. Harmonus charged forward, bringing the lower end of his staff to Azekiel's legs. Azekiel blocked the staff with ease and came in for a counter. Neither of them gave any ground, twirling their weapons at each other as if in a fast paced dance. After a few minutes, they jumped to opposite sides of the platform in unison. Harmonus decided to show his mentor what he had learned. He held his staff out in front of him, and before Azekiel could react, a bolt slammed into his chest, sending him off the rooftop into the city below.

Harmonus was shocked; he didn't think the light would shoot out that fast, let alone hit Azekiel. Harmonus figured he must not need to charge up for a quick blast. He ran and jumped off the roof after his uncle. Azekiel landed on the far side of the city, destroying two houses and a roadway. A crowd started forming around him asking if he was all right. He didn't feel like he was; he felt like he had just been hit by a mountain. He started to get up and looked up to see Harmonus running toward him. "Uncle! Are you all right? I didn't think I would actually get you! I thought you would dodge it or at least block it."

Azekiel couldn't help but let out a laugh. "I'm all right, Harmonus. That flash is much faster than I thought it would be, and it packs quite the punch. It simply caught me off guard is all."

"It seems I don't need to charge the light if I want to let loose a quick shot."

"If that was a quick shot, then I'll be sure to avoid a charged one. You are doing very well, Harmonus. Just keep practicing. The more you practice your abilities, the stronger you will become and the less time it will take to use them. That's actually what I wanted to teach you today, though it seems you may not need as much practice as I thought." They got up and started walking back toward the palace. "If you can learn to concentrate on your abilities even more, the possibilities will be limitless, just like when I showed you how to bend light to create illusions."

Harmonus thought of the day they practiced on the very same platform. He could bend light to make things disappear with a lot of concentration. He could even make the sun's light more or less intense. This thought led him to think about what his mother had said. "Uncle, do you think I may be affecting the sun?" he asked.

Azekiel seemed to be taken aback by the question and looked up at the sky for a moment. "No, but I am curious as to what the cause is. I'm sure your father will want to make sure it is not you. Your father is very uneasy about this training anyway." Harmonus nodded. If anyone was able to affect the sun, it would make sense to think it was him. Maybe he was affecting the sun unintentionally with all this training. But if that were the case, then the training would make him be able to control it more, not less. He decided to stop thinking about it; it was not helping anything at the moment anyway.

"The sun is getting low," Azekiel said, still looking into the sky with a mix of concern and worry on his face.

Harmonus looked at Azekiel with the same look. "What do you think it means?"

"I'm not sure, my gut tells me it's nothing good. Many things are changing; men have now found a way to track time."

Harmonus sat down on a bench next to his uncle. "What's the point in that?"

"They noticed that the moon travels farther in the sky at times, and then at other times travels shorter."

Harmonus nodded. "Yes, I remember. When the earth first made man, they started watching the moon, and when the moon went over the western horizon, they called it a 'day.'"

"Correct. That's something that we've adopted. But now they call seven days a week, four weeks a month, four months a season, and four seasons a year. This is all to track what they call 'time.'"

Harmonus tried to follow along, but then just shook his head. "I don't understand, why track this 'time'? What's the use of it?"

Azekiel shrugged. "I'm not sure. Men are a very curious race. Some can be selfish and cruel while others can be loving and caring. Now they are even learning how to wield teva." Azekiel looked over at Harmonus. "Perhaps they are the reason the sun has moved so much."

Harmonus hadn't even realized that the sun had moved so much. He had just looked at it a few hours ago, and it seemed the sun was moving as fast as the moon. The sun was always high in the sky, but now you barely had to look up to see it. Harmonus couldn't help but think that he was responsible for the sun's sudden change. He looked back at the moon and noticed how late it had become.

"I must get going. I'm sure Korvinus is looking for me right about now." Korvinus always enjoyed spending the late hour with his older brother, though Harmonus was never sure why.

Azekiel let a half smile touch his face. "He is becoming quite fond of you. You are a good role model for him." Harmonus smiled at the praise. Azekiel always knew how to make Harmonus feel better.

"I'm happy he is willing to train under me," Harmonus said. "Speaking of which, when did you want the training to continue tomorrow?"

Azekiel started walking to the castle baths. "Same time as usual, unless you want to go off on your own for two days again."

Harmonus smiled. "Who knows? I may be gone twice as long next time."

Chapter 2: Exile

    Harmonus meditated in his personal bathroom. Unlike humans, aggelos don't need to sleep or even eat. They have such a high command of teva that small things like hunger hold no sway over them, though they do need to meditate every so often to make sure all their needs are met. Airandrius built the castle into a small volcano and put down pathways for the lava to flow through various parts of the castle, heating the water that flowed near it for the bathing rooms. Harmonus focused on the water flowing from the fountain in the middle of the bath, making small figurines dance in the water. Satisfied with his little show, Harmonus started focusing on the light in the room. At first he started bending the light, making it so he appeared to be nearly invisible. Then he reached out, influencing the light in other places. He made the light in other rooms intensify, and then he did the same to the entire country of Nivine, making the light shine as if the sun itself had wanted to blind those that dared look into the sky. Harmonus continued to reach out further; he could feel the teva of the sun. He pulled on the sun, making it move ever so slightly closer, and then he pushed it back. He tried commanding it to go back into the high sky, but the more he pushed it, the more he could feel it affect the other teva in the land. Harmonus made sure the sun went back to where it was when he initially started. Harmonus started to become frustrated. If the sun wasn't moving, then there was another force at work here, one powerful enough to stop the light from shinning.

"Harmonus!" Harmonus jumped at the sound of his name. He was so deep into his thoughts that he didn't notice Azekiel come into the room. The sudden jump even surprised Azekiel, making him clench up. Harmonus had to take a moment to collect his thoughts. One had to be a master of stealth to catch Harmonus unaware, but Azekiel seemed to be catching him as if he were a child.

Harmonus looked up at his wide-eyed uncle. "Forgive me for startling you, Uncle. I was very deep in thought. I am surprised you are here this early; I thought we were going to start training in the after hour."

"This isn't about that. Your father is calling a meeting. I came to get you." Azekiel's voice seemed urgent, though Harmonus wasn't sure if it was because he was just startled.

Harmonus rolled his eyes. "I'm sure he can make some menial decision on his own."

"This is serious Harmonus, Abbadon killed two men." He didn't need to say anything else. Harmonus shot up and darted out of his chambers with Azekiel. Azekiel walked with an urgency that made Harmonus feel uneasy. Azekiel, like Airandrius, was always calm and in control. They always made sure never to look like they didn't have control of a situation. Harmonus tried to think of what would come. Nothing like this had ever happened before. The most that had happened was some humans starting a fight over one thing or another. They were hardly even punished unless they caused more damage or hit someone who didn't take part in the fight. Harmonus and Azekiel took a right at the main hallway, heading for the council chambers. At the main doors, there were dozens of people shouting and yelling about justice and freedom. Harmonus noticed many of the men wearing a black cloth on their wrists, signifying that they were Abbadon's men. Azekiel took another right before the main doors to the chamber with Harmonus following closely behind him. They reached a set of double doors reserved for council members going to the chambers. The two guards posted there opened the doors. Azekiel was in such a rush that he barely gave them enough time to open the doors. Harmonus hated this place more than any other place in the entire city.

As he entered, he saw that all the other members were there already. Each member stood behind his or her assigned seat. The council seats were behind a table on a balcony that stood above the actual chamber, which was a giant circle containing nothing but double doors to allow whoever was to be summoned to enter. A single window opening at the top of the chamber let light stream in from behind the lekavot's chair. The council chambers were only used when the heads of each city were brought together to discuss what would transpire in the future. The lower chamber was made in case someone would need to be sentenced by the council, an idea that Ameela had come up with. The idea seemed foolish at the time, but everyone knew Ameela's ability to see into the future; so they decided to build it out of faith.

When facing the council, Azekiel sat down to the left of an open chair meant for Harmonus. To the right of the open chair sat Airandrius, then Ameela, and then Solstier at the end of the table. Harmonus took his seat next to his father. This was the first time the council had gotten together in the chamber. Before they would always meet in the throne room to discuss what to Harmonus seemed to be menial issues.

Harmonus leaned over to Azekiel and asked, "What's this all about?"

Azekiel was about to answer but then looked over to Airandrius.

"Is my son so foreign to me, that he asks his uncle a question when his father is right next to him?" Airandrius asked. He had a deep powerful voice that echoed through the air.

"Apologies, Lekavot. I simply didn't wish to disturb you," Harmonus replied.

"I see. Abbadon decided to ignore my commands and sucked the teva out of two human men, killing them."

Harmonus felt a shiver in his spine. He knew Abbadon was power hungry, but he never guessed he would kill someone for power. "Why would he do that?"

"That is why we are here. He is being held under restraint by the guards and will be judged by the council."

"Judged by the council, or judged by you?" Airandrius glared at Harmonus. He knew what Harmonus thought about the council. He never really cared about what his father had established. All he wanted to do was just go away with his uncle and play wizard. Airandrius's eyes flashed blue with anger, but then he let it subside. He would simply have to deal with his son another time.

"Bring them in!" The doors to the lower chamber were flung open and six guardsmen walked in followed by four chained aggelos and another twelve guards behind them. Harmonus recognized Abbadon right away and then noticed Rahabul, Sodomus, and Ghamorrahk chained up behind him. They were chained together by their hands, and Harmonus noticed runes on the chains. An aggelos could break through metal with ease but not if it was magically tuned with the will of the lekavot.

This time Harmonus did look to Airandrius. "Why are the others here? What did they do to deserve chains?"

"They killed some of our guards to help Abbadon escape. If Ameela hadn't been at the eastern road, he would have escaped." Harmonus felt that familiar cold chill go down his spine. Not only did they kill humans but they also killed guards just so Abbadon could escape. What would drive one to do such a thing? There was something else about

Abbadon as well. He didn't look like himself any more. His hair was no longer silver; it was almost black. His eyes had turned black as well, and the others looked just as different.

Airandrius moved his hand up just a little, and shackles came out of the ground and attached to the chains on the four. Then the chains went back into the ground, bringing the prisoners to their hands and knees. Airandrius leaned back in his chair and brought a hand to his white beard. His voice deepened to sound like a hundred thunderous voices talking at once. "You are charged with killing without cause and breaking my commands regarding the use of teva. What say you?"

Abbadon raised his head as much as he could with the chains around his neck. He voice no longer sounded like that of an aggelos but rather like that of a serpent with a hissing that seemed to make the air chill. "You are a coward Airandrius, and you will be put in your place. You fear what little power you have, so I will show you true power to fear." Harmonus could feel Airandrius's anger rise. He may not have known how to use teva as well as Azekiel, but he was far older and more powerful than any of them. His raw power made sure they all obeyed the law of the lord of fire and life. The familiar light-blue lines started to show all over Airandrius's body as he rose from his seat.

"You think you have the power to face me, fool?" Blue fire shot from Airandrius's hand and engulfed the four chained prisoners. The guardsmen ran to the edge of the chamber to avoid the heat of the fire. The aggelos didn't scream but screeched in pain as their flesh burnt. Harmonus had never seen his father lose control of his emotions before, and now he saw the reason why. If you lost control of a power like that, you could end up burning into oblivion. Then suddenly the fire stopped, Harmonus looked up at Airandrius only to see that he was looking at Ameela.

"Do not let them tear at your heart, my darling" Ameela said, looking down at the four aggelos who were begging for death. She lifted her right hand and healed the four of them. "If we treat them like they would treat us, then what makes us any better than them?" Harmonus did respect his father for the fact that he loved Ameela with all his heart, enough to make sure that his pride wouldn't get in the way.

Airandrius sat back down and looked at Ameela. "What would you have me do, then?"

"We need to see what made them choose to do what they did."

Solstier leaned over the table. "Do you really think they will tell you what happened?"

Ameela smiled and shook her head. "Of course they won't tell me, which is why I won't ask." Ameela jumped down into the chamber and approached Abbadon. When he saw he approach, he flashed a grin showing his sharpened fangs. All aggelos had sharp fangs like felines, but his were all sharp, as if he had chiseled them to a fine point. Ameela placed both her hands on Abbadon's head, and then looked into his eyes. It was quiet for a moment, and then Ameela started screaming and fell on her back. The council shot up from their seats as she crawled away from Abbadon on her back. The guards started beating Abbadon while Harmonus jumped down to help his mother. She was shaking, and her eyes looked as if they had been shocked into fear. Harmonus touched her arm, and she flinched and drew away from him.

Harmonus turned around in a fury. "What did you do to her?"

Abbadon raised his head with the same smirk he had earlier. "I showed her true power."

It was Harmonus's turn to be infuriated. His staff flashed into his hand as he approached Abbadon. Harmonus could feel it—rage. He was going to put his staff through Abbadon's chest.

"Harmonus." Harmonus stopped in his tracks and turned around at the sound of his mother's voice. She stood up with a hand on her forehead. "Leave him be, Harmonus, we don't want to be as cruel as they are. There is no punishment that would change what they have become. These daimonion are to be banished from these lands for all time." She jumped back onto the balcony and sat down.

Harmonus thought about what would happen if Abbadon was exiled. He would kill more people to become more powerful than even Airandrius. Whether his father would listen to him or not, he had to say something. Harmonus jumped back up and sat down next to Airandrius.

"Father, if we let them leave, they will just become more powerful. We should just kill them now and be done with them."

Ameela gave a look of astonished disapproval to her son. "Harmonus, you are the light and hope of our world. Are you so willing to take their lives and drop as low as they are? Their appearance has changed because of the corruption in their hearts. Would you perform the same acts of corruption?" Ameela looked over at Airandrius. "They should be exiled from these lands until their corruption has subsided."

Azekiel leaned over the table to look Airandrius in the eye. "Lekavot, I agree with Harmonus. There is something else at work here. Abbadon had to have known what would happen if he was caught, and yet he still did it. What kind of corruption would drive him to do something like that? If we let them go, Abbadon will just become more deadly."

"Azekiel," Airandrius replied, "as my brother, you would have me kill them just so you would feel secure?"

"I will support your decision to the end, Lekavot, no matter what you choose. But if we let them go, we are responsible for any harm they do to other lands."

Airandrius looked over at Harmonus. "What of you, Harmonus? Will you forsake your father if he chooses to let them go?"

"I would never forsake you, Father, but at a minimum, we should keep them here in chains so they cannot do any more harm."

Solstier leaned forward to join the debate. "If we keep them here, they may corrupt more aggelos. We should either kill them or send them far away."

Ameela spoke up again. "We have no idea what we are dealing with. My foresight did not warn me of this, which means I cannot know what will happen. If we kill them, it could release the corrupted teva into the land. Exile is the best choice, Airandrius. You must see this."

Airandrius nodded. "Then they are to be exiled, unless any of you has something else to add on the matter." The councilmembers bowed their heads in agreement. The fate of the four betrayers had been declared. Airandrius rose from his seat again. "The four of you are to be exiled. You will be put to death if you return to the land of Nivine." He waved his right hand, and the guards took the four out of the chamber to be removed from the land. The council stayed in the chamber after the guards left.

"Are you sure we made the right choice?" Solstier asked, looking to Airandrius. "We've never dealt with anything like this."

Airandrius was still looking at the doors to the chamber. "We will find out soon enough. The council is dismissed." Everyone got up to leave, but when Harmonus got up, his father put his hand on Harmonus's shoulder. "Wait, Harmonus," he said. "I wish to speak to you—that is, if you are willing." He spoke with a soft tone that caught Harmonus off guard.

How could Harmonus say no when his father acted like that? "Of course, Father. What did you need?"

Airandrius waited until everyone left the chamber. "I know you don't really care for me, Son, but know that I care for you. I don't know what will happen to Abbadon and his followers, but I don't think anything good will come of it. We must be prepared in case they ever return."

"How much damage can four aggelos do?"

"It's not just the four of them. A lot of humans are going with them as well. Azekiel thinks they may be able to build an army someday. If they do build one, they will no doubt use it against us."

"Then why did you let them go? We could have ended it right there."

"Just because it is possible doesn't mean it is going to happen. Ameela can no longer feel their presence nor look into their futures. This leaves many possibilities open. I simply want to be prepared for the worst. You and Azekiel know the most about teva and would be the best in terms of combat. I think your specific abilities to control light and to siphon teva will prove to be better than any army. But you and Azekiel alone would not be enough to face an army. The guards are a sizable force, but they aren't well trained with teva. I would like to create a special group of men under you and Azekiel—one that would be personally trained by you and that could manipulate teva in combat. Azekiel has already agreed to help train the men, but he does not want to lead them. He thinks that role should fall to you, and I am not against it."

"This doesn't make sense. Why isn't Azekiel telling me this if you already talked to him about it? Why do we even need to create this group at all? Why not teach all the guardsmen how to wield teva?"

"Training that amount of men would take far too many years. I'd rather you train small groups one at a time. I would rather have left this to Azekiel, but he refused to take command without giving you the opportunity first."

"So you want to create a group of men able to fight an aggelos? I also assume you want my training with Azekiel to stop."

"I don't want you to do anything you don't want to. Forgive me for not being a father who was always there for you; I have a country to run. But this position will give you a place by my side, so we may get to know each other more. I do not want your training to stop; I want it to go further. You are the hope I have of defeating Abbadon if he ever stands against me. He will become more powerful; there is no denying it. I knew it would happen the moment he learned how to siphon teva just as you do. I just hope he leaves us alone."

Harmonus looked at his father. Most humans couldn't tell the difference between aggelos. They all have the same fair skin with silver hair and light blue eyes. The only difference between Harmonus and his father was in the runic lines that appeared whenever they used teva, and of course Airandrius had a long beard, while Harmonus had no facial hair. It was the first time in a while that Harmonus got a good look at his father. Harmonus nodded. "I accept my position and thank you for the opportunity, Father. I will not disappoint you."

Airandrius put his arm over Harmonus's shoulder. "I know you won't, my son." They walked out of the chambers side by side. This was the first time Harmonus had walked next to his father. Harmonus started to go to the left of Airandrius, as when walking with the lekavot, you had to walk on his left side, but Airandrius put his hand up. "No, my son. From now on, you are my right hand. You will walk on my right side." Harmonus had never gotten any affection from his father. He wasn't sure how to feel about it. Airandrius must truly be concerned if he is taking his family so close. "Meet up with your mother and tell her the news. Then meet up with Azekiel to chose who you want with you in your group."

"Yes, Father. How many did you want in this group, and when did you want us to start training? Also, did you want them to be named anything in particular?"

"You can have as many people as you feel comfortable with, and start training them as soon as you can. You may call the group whatever you wish. They are your men to command as you see fit, my son. Azekiel will be there to council you, but that is all." They walked to the front courtyard of the castle. Ameela's gardens were ripe with fruit of every kind. Ameela was on the north side of the garden picking dar'kas. She looked up and waved at them as they walked up to her.

"Well isn't this a sight—my husband and my oldest son walking side by side with each other. I should cherish this moment, as it is the first and last time I shall see it." Harmonus bent over to hug her. As tall as the aggelos were, Airandrius and Harmonus were the tallest of them. After she was done hugging her son, Ameela looked up at Airandrius for a kiss, which he granted as always. She then looked back up at Harmonus with a light smile. "I assume you accepted the position your father had for you."

Harmonus nodded. "I did."

"That's good. I'm very happy for you. Please be safe, and if you plan on allowing Airia and Korvinus into this group, then please keep them safe from harm as well."

Harmonus was taken aback by what she said. He hadn't even thought about whom he wanted to be a part of this group or what he should call the group. "I honestly haven't thought about it. I didn't even think you would let them join."

Ameela gave her slight smile again. "I think they will be the safest when they are with you. But something like that should be brought up with Azekiel. He knows best about such matters."

"I'll be sure to ask him, then. Do you think we will need this group?"

Ameela looked down at the ground and spoke with a hurt voice. "We all felt what had happened to them. I would love to think that they wouldn't do anything, but I am not sure. I know now that they are the reason for the sun coming down from the sky. Abbadon has always been power hungry, but this is different. The corruption in his heart was like a void that would never stop feeding itself until all was destroyed. He felt as his parents did when they died all those years ago, which may be the reason that he turned into a daimonion."

Harmonus looked up at the sun and noticed that it was starting to rise again. It was so hard to believe that one being could affect the sun. Then he tried to remember Abbadon's parents. "How would their death have any part in this?"

"When I entered Abbadon's mind, I felt just as I did when his parents died. There was a cold emptiness with no way to fill the void."

Airandrius finally spoke up. "Abbadon also just recently found out where his parents had died. I'm sure the tear of the world left its mark on him." Harmonus thought of the place Abbadon's parents died. No one was sure why the aggelos died, but when they did, it left a large canyon in the earth. Harmonus had to stop thinking of that place. He had an army to build.

Chapter 3: Start of the War

"Faster!" Azekiel yelled as he walked up and down a line of Harmonus's sentials. Their rune-covered, white armor glistened in the sunlight as they moved. They were swinging their raised swords across their bodies creating an *X* in the air. Since they didn't have any real threat to fight, Azekiel and Harmonus had to personally train with them to make sure they reached their fullest potential. Azekiel was by far the best swordsman, which was the reason Harmonus put him in charge of the training. But Harmonus had to watch his men and make sure that everything went well. Azekiel had been training sentials for seventy years now, and they had better and better training with each new batch. It took seven years to turn a normal man into a deadly sential warrior that could challenge the daimonion. Harmonus still didn't think that the fallen would do anything. They hadn't been seen even in neighboring lands, but the training kept his father happy.

Harmonus looked to the front of the formation to see Korvinus training with the sentials, swinging his curved blade like a master. Harmonus had named Korvinus the captain of the sentials three years before, and now he was eager to prove himself to his older brother, slashing his curved blade in each direction with near perfect precision. Harmonus walked up to Korvinus with a slight smile

"You are doing quite well, younger brother." Korvinus smiled at the praise he had been waiting for. "Azekiel is training you very well."

Korvinus nodded his head. "He wants to make sure I can take on Abbadon if we ever meet." Harmonus nodded, observing his men train with perfect discipline. Over the past seventy years they had each had to prove their loyalty and their skill to Harmonus in order to be handpicked for the sentials. Harmonus had the aggelos Belesair forge the best armor that could be made for the sentials. The helms and chest plates had runes that allowed a perfect fit for the sential who wore them. The fleeces they wore on their arms had the ability to block nearly anything with little damage to the wearer. They had cuffs on their right arms and on both legs with runes that gave them increased stamina. The officers of the sentials had small cloths that hung behind their left shoulders. All of the armor was a mix of silver and white to match their master's clothing.

"The training is all going according to plan, Hegemon." Harmonus turned around at the sound of his friend's familiar voice.

"Sylvarus, what news do you bring?" Sylvarus was the first sential trained by Harmonus. Like most men, he didn't stand quite as tall as Harmonus, but he was larger built, with black curly hair and a soft voice.

"All the cities seem to be safe and sound, but there seems to be a shadow emerging from the south."

Harmonus looked Sylvarus in the eye. "How far?"

Sylvarus looked to the southern horizon as if he could see it now. "Down in Tsalmaveth."

Harmonus shook his head and then looked out to the city walls. "The lekavot is not concerned about what happens outside our borders. Otherwise I'd have all the sentials searching for them right now." Harmonus could see the guards on the fifty-meter walls. Airandrius had the walls built around the city out of fear of the daimonion or the corrupted men. Harmonus still didn't think the daimonion would try anything, but it helped Airandrius to feel more secure. In addition to that, Harmonus also had to show Airandrius every year how the sentials were doing with their training.

Azekiel walked up to Harmonus. "Everything is going well, Harmonus. Is there anything you wanted to add to their training?"

Harmonus shook his head slightly. "No need. What of the four we sent to the southern lands?"

"They should arrive in the after hour if everything is going as planned." Harmonus nodded. He had sent them out at the request of Airandrius to see what the daimonion were up to. This was the first assignment he had given his unit since they started, and Harmonus wasn't too thrilled about the idea.

"Dismiss the men for the hour," Harmonus commanded. "They have done well."

Azekiel bowed his head and left to dismiss the men. Korvinus walked up to Harmonus and drew his blade. Harmonus summoned his staff just in time to block it. Harmonus could spar with Azekiel for weeks at a time. Korvinus couldn't handle the full force that Harmonus could bring, so Harmonus had to dial it down a notch to allow Korvinus a chance to spar with his older brother. Korvinus was very skilled with his curved sword, just as his sister was with her twin daggers. He thrust and slashed in every direction, trying to break his older brother's defense, but no matter what he tried, Harmonus was too experienced and far too fast. Even Azekiel had a hard time with Harmonus's speed, and Azekiel knew that sooner or later, Harmonus would become faster than the very light he could influence.

Then Harmonus sensed another coming in behind him. Sure enough, Airia saw her brothers sparing and couldn't resist joining in. But even with three blades coming at him, Harmonus blocked and dodged with ease. He was even able to land a few blows on his siblings.

He tapped Korvinus's chest with the tip of staff and sent him flying backward. Harmonus scolded himself for letting too much of his power flow through his staff. He could destroy large boulders with an unbelievable force of energy just by tapping them with his staff, and he had to make sure he wouldn't do that to his younger brother.

The blast dazed Korvinus, and it took him a few seconds to snap back into reality. He looked to his left and noticed the crowd they had drawn. It wasn't long till Azekiel joined in. Now Harmonus was in a full defense and had to keep giving ground. Yet even with Azekiel in the fray, they still couldn't get a single blow on him. Harmonus was just too fast for anyone to get a strike in. They switched tactics to push him to the edge of the roof. Harmonus realized what they were trying to do and flashed a blinding light that caused the three of them to shield their eyes. Harmonus knew he could easily get Korvinus and Airia, but Azekiel had far too much skill with fighting. So he decided to simply jump over them to get some breathing room. The three recovered and were ready to charge when Airandrius started clapping.

"That is quite the show. I see the three of you are keeping up with your training." Harmonus knew his father well enough to know Airandrius was talking to him. Harmonus nodded as he walked over to his father.

"What brings the lekavot to the training grounds?"

"Perhaps he wanted some action himself" Azekiel suggested. Airandrius smiled at his brother's remark. Airandrius didn't need any training. He could take on all the aggelos himself if he needed to.

"I have come to see my hegemon. The matter is very urgent, which is why I sought him out myself." Harmonus took the hint and waved his hand to dismiss any who were still on the training platform. Azekiel, Airia, and Korvinus walked over to Harmonus. If Airandrius was displeased at them for listening in, he did a good job of not showing it. "The four you sent beyond our land to the south have returned."

Harmonus's interest was peaked. "What did they find?"

"Come, we will talk while walking." They started walking down to the council chambers. "They said they found a land where the sun won't shine."

"Yes, Sylvarus told me about it already. I figured Abbadon had started making the sun set over here."

"Yes, but that's not what has me worried. On their way back, they noticed very large creatures gathering near the edge of the darkness."

"Large creatures? Like earth giants?"

"I haven't asked that yet. I wanted to come get you before anything else." They entered the council chambers and took their seats. The four sentials were down in the bottom chamber. They each put their right hands to their hearts and bowed their heads as Harmonus entered, a gesture the sentials started in order to show their loyalty to their leader. As Harmonus sat down, they looked up. Harmonus could tell his men were a little more than uneasy.

"Speak." Harmonus sounded more like his father the more he trained with his men.

The second man on the right started to speak with a slight tremble. "W-we carried out your orders, Hegemon. We went south for hundreds of leagues without finding anything, but the farther we went, the more the sun went down, until finally we reached a place of near total darkness. We couldn't go farther because we couldn't see, so we turned around. On the way back, we noticed a large number of creatures that stood at the edge of the darkness."

Harmonus wasn't sure what to think of these creatures. "What did they look like, these creatures?"

"It was too hard to see them, Hegemon. They were darker than the darkness around them and colder, making the air freeze around them. They looked like tall men with hoods over their heads, and their fingers looked more like a birds talons."

Azekiel leaned forward in his chair. "How many did you see?"

The man who was speaking looked over at his partner to the left of him. The man shrugged like he wasn't sure how to answer the question. "From what we saw, Lord Azekiel, hundreds … but we heard thousands."

Azekiel shot up in his chair. "Barely a hundred men went with the four exiled! How could there be thousands?"

"I'm not sure, Lord Azekiel. Maybe they found some men in the lower lands. But they didn't seem like men; the air around them felt like it was sucking the life out of you."

Airandrius looked over at Airia and Korvinus. "Leave us. Get the council and tell them it's urgent." As Airia and Korvinus left, Airandrius looked back at the four sentials. "Were they still in Tsalmaveth?"

The man on the far right spoke up. "No, Hegemon, they were about a hundred leagues from Vecile. They looked like they were trying to get closer but didn't want to go into the light."

The council doors flew open and the rest of the council entered. After they finished catching up, they started to decide what should happen next. Azekiel wanted to send the sentials to investigate, but Harmonus wasn't willing to send his men into the unknown without more information. Airandrius sat quietly thinking of what to do. Then he turned to his son.

"How many sentials do we have?" he asked.

"No more than four hundred."

Airandrius looked over to Solstier. "How many guards do we have?"

"About two thousand if we pull them from every town and city, Lekavot."

"Get all the guards here in the capital." He turned back to Harmonus. "Get the sentials ready to move. They will come with us to Vecile."

Harmonus gave his father a puzzled look. "Us?"

Airandrius nodded. "I want the guards here with Ameela. The other aggelos and sentials will go to Vecile. How fast can your men move?"

"They can leave immediately, but Vecile is almost six hundred leagues away. If those men are heading for Vecile, they will get there long before we will. I can leave right now and be there by the after hour."

Airandrius nodded. "Very well, but just find out what is happening. Don't do anything that could put you in harm's way." Harmonus nodded, and Airandrius dismissed the council.

Harmonus ran toward the southern city. He ran faster than ever before, creating a wave of energy that shook the trees. Before long he got to the southern city of Vecile. The city had a river running down the middle of it, with wooden houses and farms all around a stone building at the center of the town. Harmonus guessed that the stone building was a keep of some sort. He slowed down to a walk, and as he approached the city, he noticed people running around. No doubt they heard him run up and saw his distinctive features, so they wanted to get the town ready for the arrival of an aggelos.

As he entered the town, a guard with a half-cape on his left shoulder approached him. No doubt he was the leader of the town. "We are honored by your presence, my lord. How may I assist you?"

"How long has the sun been setting?" Harmonus pointed to the orange sun that was barely above the horizon. The guard looked up at the sun and then back at Harmonus.

"It's been setting for some time now. Four sentials came through the city and said they would let you know, but I didn't expect you to come down here yourself."

Harmonus looked at the approaching darkness and then back down at the guard. "What's your name?"

"Henvik, my lord."

"Well, Henvik, I need you to get everyone out of the city and send them to Nicile. And make sure that your guards report to the aggelos Solstier when they reach the city."

Henvik nodded. "Right away, my lord. What of myself?"

"You're coming with me. We need to find out what monsters lie in the darkness." Henvik looked at the coming cloud of darkness. Every instinct told him to stay away from the empty void, but he had sworn an oath, which he wasn't about to break in his lord's time of need. He gave his wife and child a kiss before sending them on their way with the rest of the city.

Harmonus walked up behind Henvik. "Don't worry, Henvik," he said. "You'll be able to catch up to your family in a few days." Henvik nodded, but somehow deep inside he knew he wouldn't.

Harmonus led the way into the darkness with Henvik close behind him. Harmonus had to bring his staff out to shine a bright light to show the way. Henvik could see his breath turn to ice and felt as if his very bones were going to freeze. Harmonus felt as if vertigo had taken him; he had to shake his head and briefly close his eyes to center himself in the darkness. He had never felt such an emptiness before; it was as if the very teva of the earth and air was gone. The fabric of space in the darkness felt as if it had never even existed. He turned around to look at Henvik. Even the light from his staff seemed faded. Henvik was standing right next to him, and yet he could hardly see him. Henvik was shivering and looking into the darkness. He looked as if he were an animal that knew it was being stalked by a predator, waiting for the beast to make its move.

"Are you all right, Henvik?"

"This darkness ... I feel like it's a malice waiting to devour us. I feel as if my life-force is being sucked from me. Forgive me, my prince, but I do not wish to stay out here for long."

"I don't wish to either." Now that Harmonus thought about it, Henvik was right. The darkness was trying to suck the teva out of them, trying to fill the emptiness of the darkness. Though it wasn't strong enough to siphon Harmonus's teva, Henvik may not be able to withstand much more. Harmonus turned around to go back but felt something. It masked itself well from Harmonus, but the moment Harmonus sensed its presence was the moment it stopped trying to hide. As it got closer, Harmonus realized it wasn't one thing but many. They were surrounded. He was paying so much attention to the dead earth that he didn't notice anything coming. He looked at up at the light coming from his staff. It was barely a glow now; the darkness was trying to completely engulf the light. He poured more of his power into his staff, and it lit up like a beacon.

A chilling hiss came as hundreds of red eyes lit up in the light. Harmonus couldn't get a clear look at any of them. Their skin seemed to be just as dark as the void they dwelled in. They all looked like tall men in hoods with four red, slit-like eyes.

"I am Harmonus, prince of the aggelos lands called Nivine. I do not wish to have any conflict, but you are approaching our lands." Another hiss came from the hundreds of beings standing before him, and Harmonus couldn't help but feel like it was a laugh.

"Harsa' vor'kul lek'has vintee'kal. Ssarka hiss duu sheer va'lu." Harmonus felt the air grow even colder as he heard their menacing tongue from the dark.

"Who here can speak with me?" A low snort came from his left.

"Iee can sspeak ... with the lord of llight." One of the men stepped out of the crowd. He approached close enough for Harmonus to realize it wasn't a man. It stood three meters tall and had a long tail that it used to whip the ground beside it. Its skin looked black and scaly, and a hood of skin went from its head to its shoulders. Its hands and feet were long with razor-sharp claws that looked like they could rip through armor. Harmonus could hear air pass through slits in its neck, creating a vile hissing sound as it breathed. Its four red, slit eyes glared at Harmonus with a burning hatred that seemed to make him forget about the cold. It grimaced, revealing hundreds of razor-sharp teeth and black, forked tongue flicking out to test the air. Whatever this beast was, Harmonus knew it wasn't peaceful.

"Why are you approaching our lands?"

The creature tilted its head as if it were amused by the question. "To make them our own. The time of the light is over; it is time for darkness to begin." The beast lunged forward and spat a yellowish liquid toward Harmonus. Harmonus quickly dodged the liquid but wasn't fast enough to get Henvik out of the way. When the liquid hit Henvik, it dissolved his armor almost instantly and quickly started to dissolve his flesh. Harmonus tried to help the guard, but the creatures were too fast. They ripped Henvik open before he could even let out a scream, devouring the man in seconds. Harmonus hardly had enough time to process what was happening before the others were nearly on him. When the first few came close enough, Harmonus swung his staff into them, cutting through them like butter. The power of his staff destroyed the creatures with ease, but hundreds more were charging toward him. He shot a bolt out his left hand, letting the crackling light disintegrate any unfortunate enough to be caught in its path. Harmonus realized he was completely surrounded. He stopped the light and began to spin his staff around his body to form an amazing globe of protection. The beasts realized they couldn't touch his zeyak, so they started spiting their yellow venom and whipping their tails in an effort to break his defense. Harmonus decided he needed to return the favor. He started charging his staff, the familiar blue lines appeared over his body, and his eyes started to glow. He stopped spinning his staff and gripped it with both hand. Then he slammed it into the ground, creating an explosion of energy that shot thunderous light in every direction, arcing from on beast to another, disintegrating them instantly. The ones that were fortunate enough not to be hit by the bolts fled in terror from the crackling light.

Then there was silence. Harmonus always liked silence, but not this kind. This was a silence of silence, devoid of life and joy. Harmonus had had enough of this silence. He tried to make the sun's rays beam through the darkness, but he couldn't prevail, at least not without burning the rest of the world. Harmonus realized it was time to get out. He tried to find Henvik's body in the darkness, but he couldn't even sense the smallest amount of teva.

"Henvik, you will not be forgotten," he spoke aloud. His words fell on deaf ears in the darkness. Harmonus built an altar at the edge of the darkness for his fallen friend and then ran back to Nicile. Airandrius had to be informed of what had happened.

Chapter 4: Death in the Family

"How many were there?" Airandrius asked. He was pacing back and forth, trying to figure out what these creatures were.

"I'm not sure. Enough to keep me on the defensive," Harmonus replied. He stood next to Azekiel in the middle of the Be'ai fields, which were right about halfway between Nicile and Vecile.

"If these beasts are fast enough to keep you on the defensive, then a normal man would be torn to shreds if he were attacked. What of the one that talked to you?"

"He ran the moment I dodged the venom, though I have no doubt that he's more important than the others."

Azekiel walked up in front of Harmonus to look him in the eye. "Do you think these creatures are Abbadon's doing?"

Harmonus nodded. "They very well could be. Even if they aren't, the dead lands definitely are. They have been depleted of all teva."

Azekiel looked over to Airandrius. "That means all the teva from the dark lands now flows through Abbadon." Airandrius turned around to look south toward Vecile.

Airia walked up next to Harmonus. "I'm glad you came out uninjured, Brother." Harmonus looked down at his younger sister with a smile.

"If I had been, I'm sure it would have been nothing you couldn't fix." Airia was almost as good as Ameela when it came to healing. She smiled at the comment and then walked up to comfort their father. Harmonus turned around to see the number of sentials they had been able to gather. They were hundreds of leagues from Vecile when Harmonus got back to them. Even though they weren't close to Vecile, Harmonus was still impressed by how fast the sentials grouped up and went on their way. Harmonus turned back around to look at his father. They were on the brink of war, and yet Airandrius didn't show any sign of fear or uncertainty.

Harmonus walked up beside Airandrius and asked him, "Do you think this will start a war?"

Airandrius looked away from the rising darkness. "I hope not, yet I feel there is no avoiding it. This will be the first time this world has tasted war, and I feel it won't be the last. Men are greedy and selfish even without corruption's influence. I'd hate to be a part of any war, yet fate, it seems, decrees that I must be the start of the first one."

"What can we do?"

"Hope ... You are the father of hope, dear son. Do you think there is any hope that there won't be a war? Or that Abbadon will end his foolish pursuit of power?"

The "father of hope." Harmonus thought back to when he had first heard this title. He was more well known as the lord of light, and he liked that title better. What can hope possibly do? Airandrius was looking back at Harmonus, waiting for an answer. All he could do was nod at his father. Harmonus didn't want to hurt what little hope they had.

"Should I go back to Vecile?" Harmonus asked. "I may be able to hold off the darkness, at least for a little while."

Airandrius shook his head. "I don't want to risk of one of them injuring you without any of us there to help. All of the people made it out, correct?"

"Yes, I passed by them on the way here."

"Good. I need you to go back to Nicile. Make sure everything is all right there."

Harmonus gave him a curious look. "What would be wrong with Nicile?"

"I don't know. The sun was starting to go down there again when we left. I'm just a little worried about Ameela. As powerful as she is, she is no fighter. I've had a very uneasy feeling since we left, and just want to make sure she is safe. I would send Korvinus, but you are the fastest by far. Just make sure everything is okay and come back as soon as possible."

"Do not fret, Father. I'm sure everything is as it should be. I'll head there immediately and give mother your love." Airandrius nodded. Now that he thought about it, Harmonus could feel it as well. It was as if those predators from the darkness were after Ameela.

Harmonus charged forward, running as fast as he could. He wanted to make sure everything was okay, but Airandrius was hardly ever wrong. If he felt like something was out of place, there probably was something. So he ran, faster and faster, until he was able to see the smoke rising. Harmonus stopped. He couldn't believe what his eyes were seeing. Nicile was razed, reduced to rubble, while lava poured from the mountain. A crash came from the far side of the mountain. Harmonus noted that it must have been the northern side of the city. At first Harmonus thought the sound was debris falling, but then he heard it again, accompanied by a scream. He had never heard that scream before, but he knew who's it was. It was his mothers. Harmonus ran toward the noise. He didn't care about any other survivors; he only cared about her. When he got to the other side of the mountain, he found his mother battling another aggelos with black hair and dark robes. Ameela brought massive boulders up from the ground and sent them down on her opponent. He dodged and smashed through them with ease, all the while getting ever closer to his target. She lifted more boulders into the air and then jumped onto one of the higher ones in an effort to evade him, but she was too slow. Her assailant drove his sword into her side. All the boulders dropped as she fell to the ground.

Harmonus charged forward as fast as he could and slammed into the man, sending him into a mountain of ruble. Harmonus charged a fierce, crackling light between his hands to finish off the attacker. When he released the light at the rubble, the man jumped above the light and came down to strike Harmonus with his sword. Harmonus deflected the attack and let the sword slide to the end of his staff, bringing the other end of his staff into the assailants head. The force of the blow slammed the cloaked figure into the ground, throwing his hood back to reveal his face.

Though his features were much darker than before, Harmonus immediately recognized the assailant as Abbadon. Abbadon snarled as he turned to flee, but Harmonus charged after him. Harmonus had almost caught him when he heard his mother screaming. Harmonus ran over to Ameela as Abbadon fled. Ameela's wound started to turn black along with her blood. Harmonus wasn't sure what to do; he was no healer.

"Mother! How do I fix this? What do I do?" He supported her head with his arm as he examined her wound. Then he saw she didn't have one wound but many. She had so many that he wasn't sure which to treat first. Ameela was gasping, trying to tell her son her last words. Harmonus had no skills in the healing arts. It takes so much just to injure an aggelos and they can heal so quickly that there was no need for him to know the healing arts until now. He hoped her wounds would start to heal like all others, but these wounds weren't healing. In fact, it looked like they were only getting worse. Ameela's placed her hand on her son's cheek so that he would look her in the eyes.

"Ab-Abbadon was trying … to take my teva. I-I didn't even sense him." She struggled as she spoke. "You are our future, my son. Don-don't be afraid."

"Save your energy. I have to get you to Airia." Ameela shook her head.

"Take my teva before the earth does. This … land will die, you have to p-protect the other lands."

Harmonus couldn't believe what he was hearing. How could she ask him to abandon these lands, and why would she ask him to take her teva? No being can survive without teva. If he took hers, then any chance of her survival would be gone. "Harmonus, you must do this." The black blood started to ooze out of her mouth. "I cannot heal these wounds."

Harmonus felt tears come to his eyes. He knew the teva was leaving her body without having to feel it. If Ameela couldn't heal these wounds, then there was no way Airia or anyone else could. He stood up and released the teva that he had trained for so long to keep inside. He raised his arms to direct the teva toward his mother. He could feel the teva leaving her to join him as a faint, blue aura formed on a path from Ameela to Harmonus.

Ameela looked up at her son and said, "I love you," With that, the final bit of teva was siphoned, and Ameela disappeared into the air. The rush of Ameela's power overwhelmed Harmonus. The amount of teva he had siphoned made his powers triple, but it hit him like a tidal wave. His vision blurred, and then everything went black.

Harmonus felt like he was adrift, like the stars above the sky. His mind was too clouded to concentrate. He could hear his name being called by a familiar voice, though he could not tell who the voice belonged to. As he started to clear his mind, the voice calling his name became louder. He knew that voice; it was screaming at him from a great distance. Harmonus woke. He was floating, along with several large boulders. He shook his head to dispel the dizziness and fell. When he hit the ground, he noticed Korvinus running over to him. Harmonus's senses were overwhelmed. It was as if they were magnified multiple times over. Korvinus finally reached Harmonus and gave his older brother a puzzled look. "Are you all right?"

It took Harmonus another moment to focus. Then he looked at his slightly shorter brother. "Mother died."

Harmonus could see the shock enter Korvinus's mind. Harmonus started to lose concentration again; it was far harder to control his powers now. If he simply looked into Korvinus's eyes, Harmonus could tell what he was thinking, so he had to look at the ground. No wonder Ameela was always so understanding.

"How?" Korvinus asked.

"Abbadon. He must have done something to his blade. Every cut he inflicted poisoned mother little by little until she couldn't fight any longer." Harmonus didn't have to look into his brother's eyes to feel the grief in his heart.

"But why? She was the only one who protected him in the council. And why didn't you go after him!"

"He was after her power. When I showed up, Abbadon ran off, and mother was dying. She told me to absorb her teva and save the land." Korvinus was soaking in what Harmonus had said. "Did Father send you right after I left?" Harmonus added.

Korvinus shook his head. "After the fourteenth moon, Father started to worry, so he sent me."

"The moon passed fourteen times!"

Korvinus nodded. "Were you floating there the entire time?"

"I'm not sure. I've never taken someone's entire life-force of teva before. I felt as if I was swimming with the distant stars in the sky, I couldn't control it."

Korvinus looked up into the sky and then back down at Harmonus. "Are you well enough travel? Father will want to know what happened."

Harmonus nodded. "Yes, let's go."

Harmonus started off at what he thought was a light jog, knowing Korvinus couldn't keep up at his full speed. He looked back at Korvinus and noticed he was moving a lot faster than Korvinus was. Harmonus slowed down to let Korvinus catch up and then kept the pace right next to him. Harmonus could feel the teva coming from Korvinus and from all over the land. Ameela had been far more powerful than Harmonus thought, and it made him feel uneasy. If Ameela was that powerful, then they had dangerously underestimated Abbadon this entire time.

"I should have killed him when I had the chance." Airandrius said, sitting down on a rock next to Azekiel. He rarely sat down when others were standing, but the news of his wife's death brought even the oldest and strongest aggelos down.

Perhaps that's why Abbadon went after Ameela first, Harmonus thought, though he didn't think Abbadon was that cunning. Then again, how did Abbadon know she was alone in the first place? He wouldn't attack her with any others around; he knew it would be suicide. Any plausible answers just led to more questions. Harmonus looked down at his father for the first time. He could sense a mixture of despair and rage within him. He was the oldest aggelos, which, in turn, made him the most powerful. But even the most powerful can be broken by those they love.

Harmonus realized that his father was looking up at him and asked, "What do we do?"

Airandrius got up and walked toward the other aggelos. "The darkness is moving away from Nicile and heading toward the eastern city of Alabask. I sent your sentials to protect the city the best they could. Do you think they can defend the city?"

Harmonus shrugged. "Perhaps if an aggelos is with them. It's obvious the creatures are weak against light, so we simply have to make sure everyone we send can summon light at will."

Airandrius nodded. "Who should we send with them?"

Harmonus wanted to go, but it would have been foolish to fight without full control of his powers.

Azekiel stepped forward. "I'll go."

Airandrius shook his head. "I need you here, Brother. I don't know what they plan to do by taking the eastern city, but I doubt it's what it seems." Airandrius looked at Harmonus. "Who do you think should go?"

Harmonus looked at Solstier and Belesair. Both of them looked like they wanted to go, but they didn't know war. The same went for Vularus and Vendiak. The most logical choice would be to send Kav'wai, though Azekiel may not approve of sending his only son to the front lines. Harmonus didn't want to send his best friend into the darkness either, but he was the best choice. "What of Kav'wai?"

Airandrius nodded in approval. Azekiel, surprisingly, nodded as well. "He is the best choice for this situation," he said. "I'll go fetch him." As Azekiel left, Harmonus looked at his father.

"You knew Kav'wai would be the best choice. Why not just send him in the first place?" he asked.

"I may be the lekavot, but you are the hegemon. I wanted to be see if your feelings affected your judgment. I am pleased to see that they don't and that you are well suited to lead the army."

"Not at the moment, I'm not. I need to retrain to hone my skills in order to make sure I don't harm anyone."

"Well, let's see what you can do. Azekiel!" Airandrius beckoned Azekiel over. The three of them walked out into a clearing. "Now that we're at a safe distance, release your teva." Harmonus paused. If he just let go, his teva would slowly siphon their teva. Airandrius must have seen the pause. "Don't fret. When you were very young, you couldn't control your teva, so everyone had to learn to block it. You will only harm us if you weaken us enough. That will be crucial when it comes to killing Abbadon."

Harmonus nodded and let his teva flow out of him. Airandrius summoned his large sword. He wielded it with one hand as if it were a wand, but from the size of it you would have thought he needed both hands. Azekiel drew both his swords and held them down toward the ground on opposite sides. Then without warning, Airandrius charged. He came down at Harmonus's left, swinging his blade with deadly speed. Azekiel charged his right, bringing both blades down onto Harmonus. If Harmonus were a fraction slower, he would have been cut down by the assault. He summoned his staff and shot up into the sky.

Azekiel smiled. "Seems like you've got a few new tricks." Harmonus wasn't sure how he was flying, but he knew he enjoyed it. His fun was short lived, as Airandrius sent a fireball at him. Harmonus knew he couldn't dodge the fire, so he used what teva he could to thicken the air around him enough to create an invisible wall. It blocked the fire, but it didn't block the shockwave, which sent him flying to the ground. Harmonus landed on his back and did a quick flip onto his feet. Before he was able to take in his surroundings, they were on him again. Harmonus shot out his staff and sent a shockwave at the two combatants. Azekiel dodged the attack at the last minute while Airandrius held out his sword to block the wave. It slammed into him with an unrelenting force, yet remarkably he was able to stay on his feet. Airandrius sent a harsh flame after Harmonus in retaliation. But Harmonus shut his eyes, and just before the flame hit him, he disappeared.

Airandrius paused and then looked over at Azekiel. "Did he run away?"

"No. When he runs that fast, you normally hear a loud crackle. It's the same noise you hear when he sends the light from his hands." Azekiel closed his eyes. After a moment he smiled. "It seems our dear hegemon has learned how to become invisible."

Harmonus reappeared in front of the two. "How did you know?"

"You aren't used to all the power you have. You tried your hardest, but I still sensed your teva, though it would be impossible to find unless you were close."

Airandrius put his hand on Harmonus's shoulder. "I'm glad to see you are learning very quickly. How are you feeling?"

Harmonus was taken aback by his father's words. Airandrius had never cared how Harmonus had felt before. Harmonus figured Airandrius wasn't sure how to act with Ameela's death. "I should be all right. It's just harder to concentrate."

"From the amount of teva you took, it's a wonder you didn't die. It will take a lot more training to get you back in control."

Harmonus nodded. He wouldn't be able to fight or lead his men if he couldn't control his own abilities. "I'll simply train harder so that I may learn faster."

"Don't train too hard. We wouldn't want anything to catch you off guard or catch you over doing it."

"Azekiel, would you see Kav'wai off for me?" Airandrius asked. "I wish to speak with my son." Azekiel nodded and walked over to Kav'wai. Airandrius sat down and beckoned Harmonus to sit next to him. Harmonus couldn't help but think that something must have happened to his father; all this behavior was knew to him. He walked over and sat next to his father.

"Son," Airandrius said, "this war is already more costly than I ever would have imagined, and it has only just begun. Ameela has been with me since the very beginning, and she was the most precious thing I've ever had. You and your siblings are all I have left to hold onto. I need your hope, my son. I need to know the three of you will make it." Harmonus thought on his father's words. He was opening up to Harmonus. Harmonus couldn't believe it; he had never seen his father so vulnerable. The aggelos are a very proud race—too proud to show any sign of weakness to anyone. Airandrius was the lord of the aggelos, which meant he had the most pride of them all. Harmonus wondered if it had all been just an act, behaving the way he did just to act the part only to show his true self to the one he loved most in this world. Now the only person he could open up to was gone, Harmonus was the one his father could talk to. He was the one his father could count on in trying times.

"Your mother had many abilities, Harmonus. She could move massive thing with her mind, she could enter one's mind to learn one's very thoughts, and she could also predict things that had yet to come true." Airandrius seemed to drift away for a moment, and then he looked back down at the ground. "Do you think she knew what would happen when we exiled Abbadon?"

Harmonus couldn't help but wonder the same thing. She had to have known, but he couldn't bring himself to think that she would release them knowing she would die. "I don't know, Father. Maybe she couldn't see what would happen if the corrupted were involved."

Airandrius's brow furrowed. "What do you mean?"

"Mother should've been able to sense every living presence of this earth, yet she told me that she didn't sense Abbadon coming. Perhaps he has found a way to hide from her abilities."

"Or perhaps she simply didn't know how to sense the corrupt. We've never encountered anything like them before."

Harmonus nodded. That would make more sense. Now that he had his mother's abilities, he could try to see if he could sense them. "Should we convene the council?"

"For what?" Airandrius replied.

"To make sure everyone knows we are at war."

Airandrius shook his head. "They already know we're at war."

Chapter 5: Beast in the Dark

"Hegemon, the darkness will reach us before the next moon." Harmonus looked down at Sylvarus. Like all sentials, he had white armor, which gleamed in the sunlight, but unlike most sentials, he had a white cloth over his left shoulder that went down to his elbow, signifying his rank as an officer.

Harmonus nodded. "Very good, Sylvarus. Is Belesair ready on the other side of the canyon?"

"He is, Hegemon."

"Good. Go back and tell the sentials to obey his every order. Wouldn't want one of them to mess anything up, would we?"

"No, Hegemon." Sylvarus turned and ran toward the right side of the canyon. Sentials were fiercely loyal to their own and to their hegemon, but unless Harmonus specifically ordered it, they would listen to no other, not even the lekavot.

"It was the last thing your mother told me," his father told him once. "She wanted to make sure they were only loyal to you, for whatever reason." I had been over two hundred moons since the death of Ameela—two hundred moons of war without any indication of who was actually winning. After rebuilding Vecile, Harmonus and his sentials drove the darkness further south into Tsalmaveth canyon. The canyon ran deep into the world, with mountain ranges flanking both sides and an eerie teva that lingered at the bottom even before the darkness. Azekiel told

Harmonus that this was the place that Abbadon's parents died; it had left a dreadful tear in the world. Azekiel and Harmonus were almost certain that this was where Abbadon was corrupted, and they couldn't help but feel that this was the place that would hold the fate of their very world. With his newfound abilities, Harmonus could feel what the threads of fate wove, but he was never sure if he was thinking of the days past or the days yet to come.

Harmonus looked up at the sky; the darkness was coming fast. He looked over at a sential officer who was awaiting his orders. "Light the torches" Harmonus said. The officer barked out a command, and then dozens of torches lit up in unison. Harmonus made sure that his men had plenty of oil for their lights. Once the darkness reached the end of the canyon, there was no telling how long it would take for the dresh'kad to reach them. They had to make sure they had enough light to last through the long reaches of the darkness. But the torches weren't just for light; along with the darkness came a chill of freezing cold air. Though the cold doesn't do anything to an aggelos, the race of man was not as hardy as his own. He had to make sure they wouldn't freeze to death before the real force came. His sentials could probably handle such harshness, but the normal men who were fighting for their right to live wouldn't be able to take it.

Harmonus watched the approaching darkness swallow the crevasse before him. He could hear his men taking deep breaths as the terror approached. Harmonus closed his eyes and reached out. He couldn't sense their teva but rather their hatred. He knew they were close. Most of the time, the dresh'kad would allow the darkness to frighten those enveloped in it and then attack their weakened prey. But not this time. The foul light-dwellers had entered their sacred ground, and they intend to purge them all as swiftly as possible. They swarmed at the very front of the approaching darkness. Harmonus knew they wouldn't let this place fall without a fight, which is why he wanted to be here himself. In a quick flash of light, Harmonus summoned his staff and held it in front of him. He made a wall of light in front of his men. Any normal being could easily pass through it, but not the dresh'kad. If one were to even touch the light, it would lose its hand.

The dark cloud slammed into the wall like a wave of water hits a cliff. The dresh'kad screeched and hissed as they ran into the wall, cursing the light and those who dwell in it.

"Belesair!" Belesair heard Harmonus roaring his name as it echoed through the canyon. Without hesitation, the sentials threw their torches into the canyon. The oil on the bottom of the canyon lit up in flame, engulfing the advancing army. Those that were fortunate enough not to be caught by the flame or Harmonus's light started scaling the cliffs on either side.

Harmonus, sensing their retreat, lowered the protective wall of light and charged his staff with electricity. The staff lit up with a blue hue and crackled in response. Harmonus held his staff above his head parallel to the ground and released the charge he had built. Over a hundred streams of thunderous light burst from his staff and blasted the cliff side, sending boulders and dresh'kad down into the flames below. Harmonus reached out, sensing those that were not close enough to be affected by the fire. Before they could retreat out of the other side of the canyon, Harmonus was upon them. His staff cut through them with almost no effort. Once they realized they were up against the hegemon, it was too late.

The darkness dissipated, and sun started to show its lovely light again. Harmonus was standing at the end of the canyon looking into the crevasse that seemed to go down into the earth and come back up on the other side. He felt Belesair approach him from behind his left shoulder.

"A well fought victory yet again, Hegemon," Belesair said. "Your plan worked so well that we didn't lose a single man."

Harmonus nodded without a hint of enthusiasm. "How many dresh'kad do you think could fit in this canyon?"

Belesair was the shortest of the aggelos. Maybe because of that, he seemed to be much bulkier. He furrowed his hard brow and brought his chin forward, making his beard point out. "I'd say about six to seven thousand. Did their ranks reach the other end of the canyon?"

Harmonus gave his usual nod. "There were more on the other side still trying to get in the canyon."

"How many more?"

"Too many. I couldn't sense the end of their ranks."

Belesair looked into the canyon. "You would think that their numbers would start to dwindle as ours have. I'm surprised there would be so many without a daimonion to lead them."

"Maybe there was and we just didn't know he was there. This canyon feeds off the living teva of everything that comes close. Perhaps once the daimonion realized that we were here, he simply fled. And with the canyon trying to drain the teva out of our soldiers, we would never have sensed a presence."

"Do you think we will be affected by this canyon like Abbadon was?"

"I'm not sure, though I do think it's best that no living thing should be around it for too long. Build a watchtower in Vecile to keep an eye on Tsalmaveth; this won't be the last time they come for the earth's scar."

"You don't want to use this canyon to pass through the mountains?"

Harmonus shook his head. "We'll go around the mountains. This place will do more harm than good if the men pass through."

"Very well. Shall we head back Varsol?"

With a nod, Harmonus turned around and looked at the sential officers. When they noticed their commander turn around, they immediately stopped what they were doing to await further orders. Harmonus flicked his wrist, and they ran off to organize the others. Harmonus couldn't help but smile. The sentials were the pride of the somewhat new Airandrian military. A single dresh'kad could wipe out a group of well-seasoned warriors, but a single sential could hold his ground against two or three dresh'kad. Their armor was imbued with Harmonus's own teva, allowing the armor to handle almost anything but a bite from the foul beasts. Because the teva was from the lord of light, their armor glowed white, much like the robes of the aggelos themselves.

Varsol was the easternmost city in Nivine, just north of Alabaster. Since the destruction of Nicile, it became the unofficial capitol of the land. The city had two sections bordered by massive walls with towers at every bend. The innermost section of the city was comprised of houses and social areas. The outer section of the city was where men and women trained to become members of the military. Outside the walls were more towers and farmland with flat fields that went on for leagues.

Harmonus and Belesair entered the city and headed straight to the council building. As usual, Airandrius and Azekiel were in the war room debating what needed to be done. The actual council chambers were rarely used anymore, which had led to a lot of issues remaining unresolved, since the council deemed them irrelevant to the war at hand.

"—elling you, we should march in full force. The daimonion and their pests cannot stop all of us." Airandrius and Azekiel seemed to be arguing about the next plan of attack.

"And I am telling you that no one has ever gone that far south before, Lekavot. We could be marching for leagues in the dead lands, and without knowing what provisions we need, it would be suicide. That's not to mention that the cities would be left unguarded. We need to find a way to lift the darkness before we even attempt to go into those lands."

Harmonus and Belesair entered the room. "Welcome back, my son. Did your premonitions prove fruitful?"

Harmonus nodded. "The dresh'kad attacked with at least seven thousand, but we repelled them." Airandrius and Azekiel widened their eyes at the news.

Azekiel was the first to ask any questions. "A force like that without a daimonion? I didn't think they had that many to waste. What of our losses? Were they great?"

Harmonus shook his head. "We had no losses; the dresh'kad fled into their lands." The two nodded in unison with approval.

Airandrius walked over to a table with a map and pointed at it. "Did you see what was on the other side of Tsalmaveth?"

Harmonus nodded. "Same thing as the land south of Vecile. The teva was drained out of everything. But the valley itself seemed different. As if a void was trying draw the teva out us. It wasn't strong enough to effect Belesair or myself, but I feared it would harm the fighters or even the sentials."

Airandrius looked over to Azekiel. "There can be no mistake; that must be where Abbadon was corrupted. Perhaps if one spent too long in that place, even an aggelos wouldn't be able to make it. Did you station any men there?"

"No, Lekavot. It's too dangerous; I do not wish to place my men in harm's way unnecessarily. I told some of the warriors to build a tower overlooking the canyon. That will give us a warning if anything happens while also keeping them far enough away."

Airandrius nodded. "If we can't go through Tsalmaveth, then we have to go through Alabaster. We have to go on the offensive before Abbadon is able to make more dresh'kad."

Azekiel hunched over the map. "That's not a good idea, Lekavot. They know that's the only way into their land. We should take a few ships and keep them out of the darkness until they can find land south of them. Then we can flank them from the south. We would be far more successful, especially with Harmonus leading the assault."

Harmonus walked over to the map. Not surprisingly, it only showed the kingdom of Nivine. The only ones who went further south than the kingdom were the exiled ones. "I don't like that plan either," he said. "What if they have the entire southlands under the darkness? We could be lost for a very long time."

"Then we should send a ship to explore at th—"

A sentinel charged into the war room. "Hegemon! Alabaster is lost!"

A shock ran through Harmonus. "What! How? What happened?"

"The darkness started approaching Alabaster again. Aggelos Valarus told me to come for reinforcements, but by the time I reached the northern edge of the city, the darkness had reached it. All I could see was the towers falling. I heard roaring and screeching from the sky. I thought it was a dresh'kad, but it sounded far larger."

"Stay here and answer any questions they have for you." Harmonus started heading for the door when Azekiel interrupted.

"Hegemon, I should come with you." Azekiel knew Harmonus would head to Alabaster, and he didn't have time to wait.

"If you can keep up," Harmonus replied. Then he shot up in the air, sending out a wave of energy.

Alabaster was the southeastern city that sat at the bottom of the mountain range that ran west to Tsalmaveth. This was the third time the dresh'kad attacked the city. Without Tsalmaveth, you had to go through or around the eastern side of Alabaster to reach Nivine. After the first siege of Alabaster, the city was rebuilt to be a military stronghold that was nothing more than walls and towers.

When Harmonus approached, he noticed the darkness wasn't as thick as usual, but the cold air was still the same. He landed in what used to be the city and reached out in an attempt to sense his fellow aggelos. Instead, he sensed another presence that seemed to sense him at the same time.

"Well, well, the great aggelos commander. I wondered when we would finally cross paths. Azekiel always spoke very highly of you." The daimonion walked up close enough for Harmonus to see who was in the dark.

"Ghamorrahk. Where is Valarus?"

"You're too late for that, Prince. Abbadon the Great already killed him. I'm here to start our next attack on Nivine." Ghamorrahk raised his arm to show his spear. It was as long as Harmonus's staff but was black. The spearhead was made of two blades that spiked outward at the bottom. It had thornlike spikes that went down a quarter of the rod. "Come forward, Harmonus. It's time to fight and see if you are truly as powerful as Abbadon thinks."

Harmonus shot out an arc of light and then shot forward, with his staff ready to cut through his opponent. Ghamorrahk spun out of the way of the light and barely had enough time to bring up his spear to block the attack. Their weapons released shockwaves of energy when they slammed into each other. Harmonus knew the battle was already over. Ghamorrahk may have been able to fight the other aggelos and maybe even Azekiel, but Harmonus was faster and far more powerful than they were. He could sense Ghamorrahk's power, and it was nowhere close to Harmonus's level.

With speed as fast as the light he wielded, Harmonus spun behind Ghamorrahk and brought the other end of his staff into his enemy's head, sending Ghamorrahk hurling forward. Harmonus ran in front of him in a flash and swung his staff from the end, smashing Ghamorrahk's head with the other end. The force sent him into an airborne cartwheel until Harmonus caught up to him again and brought his staff into Ghamorrahk's chest. Ghamorrahk smashed into the ground, creating a small crater. Harmonus was surprised to see Ghamorrahk take such abuse and still able to fight.

Harmonus went at Ghamorrahk, ready to slam his staff into his opponent yet again, but Ghamorrahk rolled out of the way and thrust his spear at Harmonus. Harmonus was impressed that Ghamorrahk was able to get out of the way so quickly, but then he realized the daimonion could hardly even stand. Ghamorrahk was crouching with one hand on the ground, waiting for Harmonus to come forward. When he thrust his spear with his other hand, Harmonus had already processed what had happened. Harmonus spun out of the way, dodging the spear. When he turned a full circle, he brought his staff into his enemy's head one last time, slamming Ghamorrahk's face into the ground. When Ghamorrahk tried to rise again, Harmonus kicked him backward. Before he could hit the ground, Harmonus grabbed his leg and swung him over and into the ground. Then he spun his staff and drove it through Ghamorrahk's back. When the end of his staff went completely through Ghamorrahk and hit the ground, it created a crevice in the earth.

Ghamorrahk screamed out "dresh'keer" as Harmonus pulled his staff out of his foe's back. Harmonus wanted just to take his teva now and be done with it, but he had to find out how Abbadon created his abominations. He turned Ghamorrahk over and looked deep into his eyes. Ghamorrahk could feel Harmonus enter his mind. He tried to stop it, but he was powerless to resist. Then Harmonus lost focus as a huge winged beast slammed into him. Harmonus brought his staff into the beast's chin in retaliation. The beast shrilled and flew into the sky as another dove down to attack Harmonus.

Though their skin looked like that of the dresh'kad, the winged beasts' skin seemed to be much tougher. As the second dove for him, Harmonus sent an arc of thunderous light at the beast. The beast let out a shrill screech that seemed like it could be heard for leagues, but it did not relent. Harmonus realized these beasts were far tougher than the dresh'kad as one came down and slammed into him. Harmonus took his staff and brought it through the beast's neck; then he grabbed the other end and spun it, severing its head. When the beast stopped twitching, Harmonus sensed three more descend upon him. He charged his staff and unleashed his crackling light at them, making sure to have enough energy to finish them. Though the blast didn't disintegrate them as he thought it would, they fell from the sky nonetheless. Harmonus looked for Ghamorrahk and realized he was calling on these beasts so he could escape.

Harmonus scolded himself for allowing Ghamorrahk to escape, but then he realized it didn't matter. The fight was over, and it was time for Harmonus to share the knowledge he had obtained. As Harmonus approached Varsol, he noticed Azekiel getting men ready for the march south. Azekiel turned around and waited for his nephew to come within speaking distance.

"Back already." Azekiel made it seem more like a statement than a question. "Is there anything left?"

Harmonus shook his head. "Abbadon killed Valarus, and Ghamorrahk is leading their forces. I'll tell you more when we reach the war room." Azekiel nodded and followed Harmonus into the inner city.

When they entered the war room, Airia ran up to Harmonus and gave him a hug. "I'm glad you're unharmed. You left in such a hurry, I didn't get the chance to ask you how the battle at Tsalmaveth went." Since Airia was more of a healer than a fighter, she always had to be with

Airandrius, Harmonus, Azekiel, or Korvinus. Most of the time she was with Korvinus doing random errands for Airandrius.

"You don't need to worry about me, Sister. I'll be fine. Where is Korvinus?"

"He should be on his way from the shore."

Airandrius put his hand on Harmonus's shoulder. "What of Valarus?"

"Killed. By Abbadon. And Ghamorrahk is the one leading Abbadon's forces."

Azekiel snorted. "Should have known. The only reason he sparred with me was for the chance of no longer being second best. Were you able to challenge Abbadon?"

"No, he was gone by the time I got there. I did have the chance to either kill Ghamorrahk or enter his mind to find out what they were up to. I chose the latter."

Airandrius frowned. "Why? You could have taken Abbadon's best tactician!"

Azekiel put his hand on his brother's shoulder to calm him down and then looked over to Harmonus. "Why weren't you able kill him after reading his mind?"

Harmonus sat down in a chair at the main war table and rubbed his temples with one hand. "Would you like me to tell you what happened, or would you rather continue asking me questions?"

Airandrius sat down across from Harmonus. Custom forced the others to sit at the table as well. Airandrius raised his hand, beckoning his son to begin the story.

"When I reached the city, it was destroyed. Ghamorrahk was there, and he challenged me to battle. After a brief duel, I brought my staff through his chest."

Azekiel leaned forward with a look of bewilderment on his face. "He must be a lot stronger than I remember to survive that amount of punishment."

Harmonus nodded. "It's from taking the teva out of the land. It seems all of the daimonion have learned the technique. When I entered his mind, I found out how they were able to create such a large and powerful force. Abbadon used the very shadow he forged from his heart and dripped his blood into a ritual that creates these abominations. That is why they cannot be in the light and why they are so loyal to their masters. Abbadon's blood gave them life, binding them to his will." Azekiel and Airandrius shared a concerned look and then turned their gaze back to Harmonus. "Because of their weakness to the light," he continued, "Abbadon mixed his darkness with the foul earth of their lands, making them much larger and more resistant to the light. Before I could get more information out of Ghamorrahk, a group of them attacked me. Ghamorrahk called them *dresh'keer*. They have long heads with razor-like teeth and feet with the same claws as the dresh'kad. Unlike the dresh'kad, however, these beast have two very large wings instead of arms. Anything too big to fit in their mouths they just ram into. With the speed they can fly at, they can topple walls and towers in moments."

Airandrius looked over at Azekiel. "How do we fight these abominations?"

Azekiel looked at Harmonus and answered, "We learn how to fly." Then turning to his brother, he added, "And create a beast that can devour theirs."

Airandrius shook his head. "How can we do that without Ameela?"

Airia, surprisingly, spoke up. "If we can't have the best"—she looked up at Harmonus—"we'll have to make do with what's next." The others smiled and nodded in agreement.

Chapter 6: Basilisk of the Light

Harmonus stood at the shores of Varsol looking out at the endless waves of the ocean. His siblings were standing behind him, staring down at rubble between them. Airia walked up to Harmonus.

"At least this one put up more of a fight, Brother," she said. Harmonus had been trying to create a creature that would rival the dresh'keer. After the dresh'keer had been created, the aggelos had started to lose more and more battles. Harmonus began creating beasts of all sorts trying to combat the dresh'keer. He created beasts ranging from serpents of the sea to goliaths of the earth, but over the past two years, he had yet to create a beast that could rival the abominations. The only ones that could bring down the mighty beasts were the aggelos, though it came very close many times. The Airandrius family couldn't be everywhere at once, so they decided to stay at the eastern city of Varsol, spearheading the attacks from there. But with the most powerful aggelos in one place, the darkness was able to consume Vecile and the land to the west. Though no aggelos had died since Valarus, they were still losing the war. The aggelos couldn't live in a dead land. This was why Harmonus's work to create a beast was so vital to the war effort.

Korvinus walked up to Harmonus. "This one was a lot tougher," he said. "What enchantments did you put on him?"

"None. I made his skin out of a tough crystal from the earth. The crystal took an immense amount of pressure to create."

"Well, at least it looks beautiful, especially in the sunlight." Airia looked at the crystal rubble with awe as it reflected the sun's rays.

Harmonus snorted. "Beauty won't hold back the abominations. Anything light enough to fly isn't tough enough to take on the beasts, and anything tough enough is too heavy to fly."

Airia turned to look at her older brother. "What about the serpent of earth Father helped you with?"

Korvinus's eyes shot up at the memory. "That serpent was an excellent challenger, especially when it sent balls of flame from its mouth. I thought for sure we had something that could challenge the dresh'keer."

Harmonus shook his head. "That beast was powerful, but it couldn't handle its own abilities. The teva can't come from two different aggelos; if it does, it will start to destroy itself."

"Then ask Father for his fire," Airia said. Harmonus looked down at his sister, stunned at the suggestion. She shrugged her shoulders when he looked at her. "It wouldn't hurt to ask."

Airia was almost cute with her communication, but if Airandrius even allowed Harmonus to take his fire, it would leave him far weaker than what he is now. Harmonus pondered the matter, and then decided he should at least bring it up. The moon had hit the western horizon. it was time for a war meeting anyway.

Harmonus entered the war room. A map of Nivine was laid out over a large round table in the center of the room, and there were ten chairs around the table. Airandrius and Azekiel were already in the room, as usual, but no one else had arrived yet. Harmonus, Airia, and Korvinus entered the room and took their seats. Airandrius always sat down at what seemed like the head of the table with Harmonus at his right hand and Azekiel at his left. As the others entered, they all took their normal seats. Airia would sit next to Harmonus with Korvinus on the other side of her. Belesair would be next to Korvinus with his son Solstier on his other side. Then would be Vendiak and Kav'wai, and Arnakia would be next to her husband Azekiel. With all ten of the aggelos together, they could decide what to do about the oncoming darkness.

After they took their seats, Harmonus had to receive the reports of the war. "What news from Kendel?" he asked. After the fall of Vesil, Harmonus had made sure there were at least two aggelos in each city He sent Vendiak to the western city of Alserel with Belesair and Solstier. Arnakia and her son Kav'wai were sent to the northern city of Kendel. That left Airandrius, Azekiel, Harmonus, Airia, and Korvinus in the frontline city of Varsol.

"Defenses are being built as planned, Hegemon, but no other news from the northern city," Arnakia replied. She was not a fierce warrior like her husband, but she was able to make sure everything happened on schedule.

Harmonus turned to Belesair. "What of Alserel?"

Belesair didn't answer with the enthusiasm that Arnakia did. "The darkness is slowly coming from the south, Hegemon. I sent my best warriors to halt it, but none have returned."

Korvinus leaned forward. "Why would the darkness come slowly?"

Harmonus looked at the map and answered his brother's question. "It means they are moving a large force, and they want to meet us in open battle."

Azekiel nodded in agreement. "Abbadon may finally have the numbers he needs, and he knows if he charges too fast, it will force all of us to meet him head on. He knows if he moves slowly, we won't send our full force because doing so would make it too easy for him to charge in from Alabaster and take Varsol."

Harmonus set his forearm on the table. "Which he still may do. Kav'wai, I'm sending some sentials to go with you, Vendiak, and

Belesair. While Solstier fortifies they city, you three do your best to slow the darkness with the warriors under your command. But if the darkness proves too strong, retreat. We cannot lose any more aggelos if we intend to win this war."

Airandrius looked over at his son, his face devoid of any expression. "Do you really think we can still win this war, Hegemon?" The entire table looked at Harmonus. If the father of hope didn't think it was possible, then it wasn't.

"Nobody ever truly wins in a war," he said. "We have to survive. If we outlast our opponents, then it will be our victory, though it has already proven to be a very costly victory." Airandrius nodded in approval and then flicked his wrist to dismiss the council. Airandrius, Azekiel, and Harmonus were the only ones to stay in the war room as usual.

Azekiel put his hand on his nephews shoulder. "You're turning into a very good leader, Harmonus. Your mother would be very proud."

Airandrius turned around at the thought and put his hand on his son's other shoulder. "She was already proud of you. Perhaps a day will come that Harmonus the wise will be lekavot."

Harmonus wasn't sure what to say. His father had never given him such praise before, and he didn't want to ruin the moment. He decided now was the best time to ask. "Father, remember when we first started creating the beasts to fight the dresh'keer, and we used both of our tevas to create one powerful beast?"

"Yes, I remember it couldn't handle both of our tevas and destroyed itself."

"Airia gave me an idea. Would you be able to give me your lordship of the flame?"

Airandrius took a step back. "You realize you are asking for the very base of my power, Harmonus. If you were able to siphon it from me without killing me, it's possible I would no longer be able fight the darkness, and then Abbadon would surely kill me."

"We are losing this war, Father. Every league the darkness moves is another league devoid of all teva that we can never use again. I would not ask this of you if the situation were any different, but if I command both our tevas, then the beast that I create won't destroy itself."

"Are you sure that your creatures will be able to stop the darkness if you have the flame?" Azekiel asked. He seemed to think the risk was worth it; otherwise he would've asked a different question.

"No, I can never be sure anymore. I simply hope it will work."

Airandrius nodded his head. "Very well, I will concentrate my power so it should be easier for you to take it. But the moment you have the flame, stop siphoning, or you could kill me." Airandrius's eyes lit up with a light-blue hue. Swirling blue lines started to form down his right arm as he raised it to summon the flame. When his arm was fully extended, he flipped his palm up, and a bright white flame appeared. Harmonus felt that the flame could rival the heat of the sun if Airandrius wanted.

Harmonus reached out with his right hand and allowed his natural ability to flow through him. Airandrius ground his teeth as his power was being torn from his hand. The white flame looked as if it were slowly jumping over and Harmonus's hand were catching fire. Harmonus could feel the power surging through him. At first it was a rush, and then it turned into a flood that burned Harmonus's very core. Harmonus closed his eyes as he tried to control the power building inside him. He could feel his light-blue eyes burning through their eyelids and the blue, swirling markings appearing all over his body. Airandrius collapsed when the flame was gone. Azekiel wasn't sure if he should help his older brother get to his feet or if he should try and help Harmonus try to gain control of his new power. Harmonus was shaking with his head looking up at the roof of the building. He clenched his fists to stop the trembling as he lowered his head. The blue markings started to disappear as he began to gain control, and Azekiel started helping Airandrius up when he determined that Harmonus was fine.

Harmonus opened his eyes to see Azekiel supporting Airandrius. After a brief moment, Airandrius was able to stand on his own. He walked over to Harmonus and put his hand on Harmonus shoulder. "How do you feel?"

Harmonus was again taken aback by his father. He was the one barely able to stand, and he asked if his son was all right. "It may take a little time to get fully accustomed, but I should fare well. What about you?"

Airandrius nodded. "I'll be all right. It didn't take nearly as much out of me as I thought it would, which means I should still be able to stand against the daimonion if the occasion calls for it."

"That is far more likely now that you are weaker. I do not think it's best to let anyone know of this; news that the lekavot is weaker would only encourage our enemies to attack at every opportunity," Azekiel said. He was always the wise thinker. Harmonus and Airandrius nodded in agreement.

With his new power, Harmonus started working on his beast. Airandrius and Azekiel even made sure to watch as Harmonus started gathering materials for the beast's creation. Harmonus carefully drew a circle of runes in the earth with his staff. He had to make sure the staff was barely touching the ground, otherwise he would crack it. Then he drew swirling marks into a smaller circle in the middle.

Airandrius had already seen this before, but Azekiel was staring with wide eyes. "What are the circles and runes for?"

"The circles allow my teva to channel through the ground more precisely, and the runes are for the name, just like on our zeyaks. They describe what the creature will look like." Harmonus reached his hand out toward a large crystal, and it flew straight into his hands. "This is the toughest material in the earth; this will be the egg for the creature. I learned that these beasts have the same skin as their eggs." Harmonus put the crystal in the center of the circle. Then he bit the side of his finger to draw blood. "The blood will bind the beasts to my will just as the dresh'kad are bound to Abbadon." Harmonus blew the flame of his father into the crystal. "He'en bak uun de ah se'av duran … harvos!"

With the old aggelos words commanding the crystal to life, the creation was complete. The crystal broke open like a bird coming from its shell. The small creature was about the length of Harmonus's arm from its horned head to the end of its lengthy tail. It had four muscled legs that it already walked on, feeling the dirt between its talons. Its white scales reflected the light with a majestic beauty, though they looked to be hard as stone. Its long snout sniffed the air, smelling every scent within a hundred leagues, and then it let out blue flames from its mouth as it exhaled, showing its long, razor-like teeth. Its large, yellow eyes took in their first sight of the world through slit pupils. Its long neck allowed it to turn its head in any direction without moving its body. The tiny beast spread its wings out, making it look many times larger than its actual size. Harmonus marveled at the sight of his creation and then knelt down beside it.

"That's it?" Harmonus and Airandrius shot their attention over to Azekiel, who had decided to interrupt the birth of the creature. "I thought you'd create something bigger to fight off the darkness."

Airandrius smiled at his brother's tease. Harmonus looked back down at the beast and said, "It will grow."

Chapter 7: Harvos

    Silent and low with his sword to the ground, Korvinus did his best to hide in the tall grass, but it was nearly useless to try and hide from this beast. Korvinus caught a glimpse of the beast in the air and looked up in a vain effort to spot it. Harmonus shook his head as he watched his brother. The *harvos* had bright and gleaming scales, which they used to reflect the sunlight and blind their enemies who were foolish enough to look into the sky. With that very thought, it happened. Korvinus rubbed his watery eyes as he ran from the whirlwind created behind him. He opened his eyes just in time to see fire rain down at him. It was too late to try to dodge the flame. He leapt forward as high and fast as he could, but he jumped too high. The beast immediately found the intruder in his territory. The twenty-meter-long beast turned and slammed its long tail into Korvinus, sending him into the ground, where he created a small hole on impact. Before he could get up, the beast landed on him, rearing its head to deliver a flame that would melt its prey in moments.
    Harmonus raised his hand. "Enough." He walked over to Korvinus with Airandrius, Airia, Kav'wai, and Azekiel behind him. The harvos got off Korvinus and sat down next to him in a playful manner. Harmonus walked up to the beast first and set his hand on its snout. "Well done, Abrox." Abrox bowed his head at the praise of his master.
    Korvinus stood up with a defiant look. "I hardly consider that a fair challenge, Harmonus! Abrox can fly faster than I could hope to run."

Airia walked up to Korvinus. "Harmonus taught us how to fly; you didn't have to run."

"He hasn't taught us how to fly as fast as his harvos."

"That's your own fault; he can't teach you to fly faster. You should be proud of the fact that he taught you at all," Airia replied.

"I'm his brother," Korvinus countered. "He has to teach me, just like he has to teach you."

Azekiel stood to the left of Harmonus. "Korvinus, this challenge wasn't to see how strong you are but to see how strong Abrox is. We need to make sure the harvos can face not only the dresh'keer but also the daimonion." He looked up at the shining beast. "I think he's ready."

Harmonus shook his head. "He may be ready, but the others are not. It takes a lot to create a harvos, and I've only been able to create two others since Abrox. Three will not be enough to vanquish the darkness."

Airandrius stood at Harmonus's right. "Right now were aren't concerned with vanquishing the darkness, Harmonus. We just need to halt it for the time being."

"I know that, Father, but Ibrex and Ilsox are just learning how to control their fire breathing. Abrox is the only one capable of fighting, and he isn't as big as I want him to be."

Azekiel looked up at Abrox. "How big will he get?"

"Harvos will never stop growing, but they will grow slower as they age."

Airandrius turned so his entire body faced Harmonus. "Harmonus, we need these beasts now. With Belesair and Vendiak gone, Abbadon has even more incentive to strike."

"I understand, Lekavot, but if I send the harvos into battle before they are ready, we will lose any chance of surviving this war. I need time to create and train more."

"We may not have that much time, Son. With the west gone, Varsol and Kendel are all that's left, and the darkness approaches with each passing moment ... How much time do you need?"

"At least another year. By that time I'll have a few more as well."

"That's far too long, Son. We need them with the other aggelos now."

Harmonus shook his head. "No other being can command them, Father. They're not like the sentials. They are bound to my blood, making them bound to only my commands. They have to truly love a being to even listen to it, even if I order them to."

Airandrius tightened his jaw as he closed his eyes. "Very well. You may not get a year, but we will give them as much time as we can spare. In the meantime, I need you on the front lines to show Abbadon we can still bite back."

Kav'wai put his hand on Harmonus's shoulder with a smile on his face. "At long last we get to fight side by side, my old friend. I'll be sure to let you kill a few before I handle it."

Harmonus looked at his friend with a smirk. "Will you now? What will happen when I kill more than you?"

Kav'wai shook his head as he walked over to speak with Airia, adding, "I won't have to worry about that."

Azekiel beckoned Harmonus to follow him and Airandrius to the war room. Harmonus nodded at Abrox before he left to let Abrox know he was dismissed. When he arrived to the war room, Arnakia and Azekiel were on the far side speaking softly. Airandrius was standing next to the main table, looking over a map.

Airandrius noticed Harmonus walk up to him. "The darkness has taken all the land west of Varsol. They will probably attack Kendel within a few moons." Harmonus sat down in a chair, and Airandrius did the same. "Harmonus, we have to do something. Perhaps it's time we all go into the darkness and try to seek Abbadon out."

Harmonus shook his head. "You are the one they are after, Father. They would ignore us and go after you. They know the men would lose the will to fight if you fell, and killing Abbadon won't end this. We have to kill every one of them to lift this darkness."

"Perhaps we should have a final fight and be done with it. They have destroyed far too much already, Harmonus. The men won't have enough land to farm in order to eat. Even if this war ends now, we have lost too much. The men will starve to death, and the aggelos will never again know the glory of their kingdom."

"Do not lose hope, Father. We will survive this, and we will rebuild the kingdom, if not on these lands, then on others. And we will kill any that get in the way."

"You truly think that could happen? Tell me something, Harmonus: as my son, are you willing to kill even me for the greater good? Are you willing to fight an endless horde for the smallest hope of peace?"

Harmonus looked into his father's eyes and for the first time saw a fear that seemed like it could tear the world apart. Airandrius didn't think we would win this war and wondered what would happen if we did. Would there be peace? Harmonus thought about peace; for such a simple word, it was an impossible thing to achieve.

"Peace is an impossible thing to have anymore, Father," Harmonus said. "It's such a strange thing, to fight for peace, but until the threat of peace is gone, I will continue to fight.

"And what of me? Will you strike down your own father or brother for the sake of peace? How far will you go to achieve your victory? How much does it take to become just as corrupt as our enemy?"

Harmonus thought on his father's words. Airandrius was in a dark place right now, and if Harmonus didn't chose his words carefully, his father's hope could be lost.

"I would never wish to fight against you, Father," Harmonus said, "but I will do what I must to protect the hope for peace."

"I suppose that is the most I can ask of you, my son. You are the only thing that can truly stop this corruption."

Harmonus wasn't sure how to react to his father's abnormal behavior, so he just nodded. Azekiel finished speaking with his wife and walked up to the table. "With your permission, Hegemon, I will send Arnakia with Kav'wai to the south."

Harmonus made a gesture with his hands in approval. "What news of the darkness?"

Airandrius pointed down at the map. "Nothing from the south, but it's approaching Kendel from the west."

"I will go there, then, and make sure to halt the darkness. Kendel is just as important as Varsol, and we cannot afford to let the city fall."

Airandrius looked at Azekiel and then back at Harmonus. "How is Kendel just as important?"

"Varsol may be the best fortified city," Harmonus replied, "but Kendel sits on the northern beach. If we cannot stop this darkness, the endless waters may be our only hope of survival."

"Very well. hall Azekiel accompany you there?"

Harmonus shook his head. "Azekiel needs to be at your side at all times. When Ghamorrahk finds out that I am in the north, he will no doubt try to test you."

Azekiel gave Harmonus a puzzled look. "You don't think he is up north?"

"No. He likes to attack fast with a small group before his enemy is ready. Whoever is leading the northern darkness likes to move slower with a full force. I will have Solstier accompany me; I am sure he would like to know who killed his mother and father."

"What of your harvos?"

"Keep them here for now. They seem to like Airia's tender care. They will be more inclined to listen to her." With that, Harmonus made a slight bow toward his father and started heading to the northern city of Kendel.

Chapter 8: Sacrifice

Solstier stood in the giant red tree on the highest branch that could hold him. Harmonus was slightly above him to the right, staring at the approaching darkness, floating motionlessly above the thick forest with his arms down at his sides. His hands were open as he made the crackling light between his fingers. The same blue markings appeared over his body as he charged his abilities, waiting for the darkness to reach them. Solstier felt as if the very earth was about to split in half at Harmonus's command. It was as if he wanted those in the dark to know of his presence. Harmonus began to speak into the wind, too silently to hear at first. Then Solstier heard Harmonus's voice in the wind, which carried it into the darkness.

"Halt your advance, and you shall live; continue, and you will all die."

Solstier looked up at Harmonus and then turned to look at the city. "If I may, Hegemon, why are all the sentials in the city?"

Harmonus answered without averting his gaze. "One hundred sentials will do no good out in this forest, especially since I plan to use it against the darkness." Harmonus waited a moment and then looked down at Solstier. "It seems they will not cease their advance. Hold on to that tree; I'll try to make sure it stays put." Harmonus's staff appeared in his right hand. He whirled it above his head, turning the air into a spinning vortex that sucked everything into it and launched it back out.

Once Harmonus was satisfied with its size and speed, he swung his staff around him until it stopped, pointing at the darkness. The vortex shot forward at its master's command, hurling trees and boulders into the darkness as it advanced.

Solstier could hear the debris smashing into any beast unfortunate enough to be in the way. Some were picked up and thrown into the light, disintegrating them in moments. Harmonus then summoned a fire in his hand and sent it into the ground before them, turning the forest in front of them into a wall of flames. But even the harshest flames were snuffed out when the darkness approached. Harmonus shot into the ground, unleashing a wave of energy that sent any dresh'kad in its way into the ranks behind them. Solstier drew his daggers, leaped to the ground, and waited, ready to fight what lurked in the darkness.

Harmonus wasn't as patient. He charged into the dark with a speed that made the air split. When he was close enough to see the dresh'kad, he thrust out his staff, sending another wave of energy. Those close to him disintegrated, and the ones behind were pulverized and flew into the oncoming ranks. By the time the dresh'kad realized Harmonus was in front of them, it was too late. He moved faster than they could see, sending bolts of light and fire through the ranks. Harmonus could sense that fear was gripping his enemy, a fear that he had felt in his father. They didn't expect their enemy to be this powerful, and they would rather face the judgment of their master than face the wretched lord of light. Once they realized what they were up against, they began to flee, ignoring their master's commands. But Harmonus wasn't done with them just yet. He had already decided to let a few get away to spread the fear, but those that had not already left would be killed. As he tore through the ranks, he found what he was looking for: he felt the presence of another.

Before Harmonus could look for the presence, Solstier started to yell for Harmonus. When Harmonus found Solstier, he was screaming. A tall, dark-haired daimonion had his axe in Solstier's chest. Harmonus shot forward, bringing his staff into the daimonion's face. The daimonion was flung through the darkness out of Harmonus's sight. Harmonus hunched down to check on Solstier but was interrupted before he could speak. "It's Rahabul. I-I'm fine. Don't let him get away."

The darkness thickened, and a wicked voice came through the air. "Do not cry, child, for I shall deal with you as I have your parents."

Harmonus rose to his full height. "Come, Rahabul. It is time for you to come into the light."

"You are certainly as powerful as they claim, Harmonus, but I have the teva of two aggelos—a power even you cannot fight."

"Then come forward and finish this. I don't know why you daimonion like to talk. I'd rather just finish you off and be done with it."

Harmonus twisted as a large axe came at him from behind. In doing so, he brought his elbow into Rahabul's face. Harmonus tried to drive his staff into Rahabul while he was off balance, but Rahabul was too quick and deflected the attack. Harmonus tried again; this time he brought the bottom of his staff up in an attempt to uppercut. Rahabul deflected the attack and brought his axe down with amazing speed. Harmonus dodged the axe in the last moment, which forced him to back up. Harmonus paused; even Azekiel wasn't this fast. With the teva of two other aggelos flowing through him, Rahabul could move almost as fast as Harmonus. Harmonus decided to take a new tack. Blue lines lit up his body as he allowed his teva to go unchecked. He shot into the air with a thunder. The total darkness made it impossible to see, so he closed his eyes. He didn't need to see his foe; he could feel him.

He shot past Rahabul from every direction, forcing the daimonion to stay on the defensive. Though he couldn't break through, Harmonus kept pushing his opponent from every angle. He sent the thunderous light from one angle as he brought up the very earth to smash Rahabul from another. Then he found the opportunity he needed. Rahabul jumped out of the canyon Harmonus created to try to smash him, but he jumped too high, making himself vulnerable until he reached the ground.

Harmonus flew underneath him and brought the tip of his staff into Rahabul's chin, sending him higher into the sky. Harmonus flew above him, charged his staff with a force that could shatter the earth, and smashed his staff into Rahabul's head, sending him into the ground. Rahabul may have been faster than Ghamorrahk, but he was neither stronger nor tougher. The blow nearly killed him, leaving him weak enough for Harmonus to finish off.

Harmonus landed next to Rahabul as he was trying to crawl away. "It's over, Rahabul. You picked the wrong side."

Rahabul stopped crawling and turned onto his back. He knew he couldn't get away. He tried to fake a smile as he spoke. "You think we've lost Harm-mon-monus? You could kill every one of us on your own and you would still l-lose. You have n-nothing left … to fight for. And once Abbadon is done with this land, h-he will consume the rest."

Harmonus tightened his jaw. "What are you talking about?" he asked. Rahabul tried to laugh but couldn't, and he slowly shook his head in response. "So be it," Harmonus said. He held his staff horizontally in front of him, bringing a red mist out of Rahabul into the staff. Rahabul arched backward in pain as Harmonus sucked the teva out of him. He tried to let out a cry of pain, but it was too late. He disappeared as the last bit of teva was drained out of him.

Harmonus felt the rush of the teva flow through him as he dropped to his knees. The darkness seemed clearer, even though it didn't change. He could feel a presence rushing at him; then he felt another. Harmonus couldn't move; the teva wasn't done settling in. His blue lines were bright enough to make it seem like the teva was breaking out of his body, a beacon for the two strangers to charge at. He closed his eyes in an attempt to regain control and then opened his eyes to see Abbadon charging at him. He was getting ready to kill Harmonus while he had the chance, and Harmonus couldn't do anything about it. Abbadon kept charging forward like a predator sprinting toward its prey. Harmonus was dead; he was sure of it. Abbadon had patiently waited for his prey to be vulnerable, and he knew that that would only be after Harmonus took a high amount of teva from his foe.

When Abbadon got within range, he leapt forward with his long blade ready for the blow. Right when he was about to get Harmonus, the second presence tackled Abbadon. Harmonus could see that it was Solstier. He knew he couldn't take Abbadon, but still he didn't hold back. Harmonus knew Solstier wouldn't last long; he had to get back in control. He trembled as he rose to his feet. His foggy mind started to clear, letting him concentrate in order to pierce the darkness. Once he was able to regain his composure, he started heading for Solstier only to see that he was too late. Solstier was on his knees. Abbadon slit his throat, sucking the teva out of Solstier as he did it.

Rage. That was all Harmonus could feel, and it was enough to gain complete control of his teva. He shot forward at Abbadon, charging his staff with enough energy to destroy a city. Abbadon was too smart to try to block that directly. As he knelt down, he swung his sword into an uppercut to divert the staff's course. Harmonus spun around in an effort to keep the momentum of his charge in motion. He swung his staff down at Abbadon just as Abbadon came back up to get Harmonus in his torso. When their weapons clashed, a loud clap of thunder went through the air, and both warriors flew back from the blast. Abbadon quickly closed the gap. He was far smarter than the other daimonions;

he made sure to stay very close to Harmonus to make his staff less maneuverable. That also made Abbadon's blade less effective, though it did not make as large a difference for him as for Harmonus. Harmonus held his staff to his chest as he looked up at Abbadon's smiling face. Harmonus felt the heat of rage fuel his abilities. He took in a deep breath. Abbadon tilted his head in curiosity, losing his smirk; there was never a need for any aggelos to take a breath. Suddenly Abbadon was engulfed in bright, blue flame, causing him to scurry.

Harmonus couldn't keep his fire breath going for long. Aggelos don't breathe like men do, so he didn't have a need for a large lung capacity. The second he stopped the fire, Abbadon fled, and Harmonus pursued. But Harmonus was in Abbadon's land now, and even his enhanced sight couldn't help him see Abbadon. He had to sense the betrayer's presence and course. Harmonus flew high into the sky and closed his eyes. For a moment all he could sense was the cold darkness, the endless void. Abbadon seemed to be far more clever than Harmonus thought. The darkness cloaked not only the sight but the mind as well, making it extremely difficult to sense the teva of another life form. But there was one part of the void that seemed to stick out more than any other: Tsalmaveth.

Harmonus quickly flew to Tsalmaveth in a futile attempt to find Abbadon. He couldn't feel Abbadon, but he could definitely feel the darkness thicken, as if the very air around him wanted to strangle him. Then he could feel it. For some reason, he couldn't feel it before, but he could now. The canyon felt like a hungry carnivore, like a void that couldn't be filled even with the death of the earth. It was an abomination in the land, a scar that would never heal. A fear entered Harmonus that he had never felt before. Something had happened the day Abbadon's forbears died, something that the very earth feared.

When he got close enough, Harmonus noticed thousands of dresh'kad lurking in the canyon. Harmonus's fear was replaced with a burning, white rage. He summoned his staff and charged at them with his thunderous light. He released it into the dresh'kad, catching them completely unaware. He smashed into the ground, sending those close by into the cliff side. Harmonus could sense their surprise, their fear of total annihilation, and ... something else. Those foolish enough not to run were engulfed in his breath of blue flames. He shot through their fleeing ranks, tearing them apart. No matter how many he killed, though, Harmonus could still feel the darkness pushing him, willing him to become a part of the endless void. But the more the darkness pushed, the harder Harmonus fought, until finally, all those that had dared to test him in battle were dead. Those that were fortunate enough not to encounter him had fled.

The land was quiet once more, permeated by a silence that seemed to be worse than the loudest noise. The void was calling to him, waiting to leech all the teva he had until he was no more. Harmonus was about to leave when he heard the wind whisper. At first it was a light breeze that sounded like a shrill screech; then it turned into a freezing wind that came from every direction. Harmonus could hear a voice in a darkness that seemed to be coming from the wind.

"You truly are powerful, Lord of Light." Though the voice seemed to be coming from the wind, it wasn't shrill. It was a deep, menacing voice that sounded as if it came from the very foundations of the earth. "To make the dresh'kad fear something more than myself is a feat in its own."

Harmonus tried to reach out to find out where the voice was coming from, but it was as if the voice came from every direction at once. "Coward!" he shouted. "Show yourself and you'll see how powerful I am. I must say, you got here quicker than I thought, Abbadon."

The voice's laugh echoed through the canyon, leaving a foreboding ache in Harmonus's stomach. "You will have your fight, young one, but it will be when I choose it and not a moment sooner." The wind fell silent, and Harmonus knew there was nothing more he could do. Abbadon would hide as he always did.

Chapter 9: The Great Shall Perish

"It doesn't make any sense!" Airandrius was pacing back and forth, trying to understand what had transpired. Azekiel sat at the war table like he always did, rubbing his beard on the side of his face. Harmonus sat across from Azekiel, waiting for his father to finish his rant. "If Abbadon was running from you, why would he even say anything?"

Azekiel sat his hand on the table. "How was he able to talk to you without you sensing him?"

"That isn't what bothers me," Harmonus said. They both looked at him. "What bothers me is how he was able to travel to Tsalmaveth so quickly. He could have used some trick or spell to speak to me from afar, but I sensed him at Tsalmaveth! How did he get there so fast without causing the air to roar?"

After a moment Azekiel stood up. "Those answers will have to wait. The real question we need answered is the one about the possibility of there being other lands. Do you think he was telling the truth?"

Harmonus leaned back in his chair. "It's hard to tell. Either way, we need to find out, because Ameela mentioned it as well. We should start constructing a vessel that would be able to handle the endless sea."

Airandrius walked over to Harmonus. "Airia and Korvinus could do that in the northern city." Unlike Harmonus, Airia and Korvinus were not very effective in war, and Airandrius knew it. This plan would not only keep them safe, but it would also make sure the job was done right.

"I'll leave about fifty sentials there as well to help and protect them, just in case," Harmonus said. Airandrius and Azekiel nodded in agreement. Kendel was built on a bay with high mountains to the north and a large forest to the west. It was nearly a straight shot north from Varsol over the Trokaen Hills. The Trokaen Hills were lush, green rolling hills and pastures that run from the sea beach to the western forest. The hills were neither tall nor long, making them very easy to pass over. If the darkness took Varsol, it would have no difficulty reaching Kendel.

"I will also send Ibrex and Ilsox up north as well; they will do no good here," Harmonus added.

Azekiel gave him a puzzled look. "Not Abrox?"

Harmonus shook his head. "We won't be able to fight the dresh'keer without him. I didn't sense any at Tsalmaveth, which means they must all be ready to charge from the south. Abrox may not be at his full potential yet, but he is ready to fight alongside his master."

"When do you think Ghamorrahk will charge?"

Harmonus was about to answer when he heard Kav'wai yelling outside. The others must have heard it as well, because as Harmonus turned around, Azekiel charged out to see what happened. Harmonus and Airandrius looked at each other and ran up behind Azekiel. When they reached Kav'wai, he was just inside the entrance to the city. He had cuts all over his body that didn't seem to want to heal. Harmonus immediately concluded that Kav'wai had fought with a daimonion. Their weapons were not only strong enough to pierce the skin but also had some dark teva that made it very hard to heal. Harmonus looked around for Arnakia only to realize what must have happened.

Azekiel screamed at the news of his wife's death. She sacrificed herself to save her son, who now collapsed in his father's arms. Airandrius yelled for Airia; she was Kav'wai's only hope for survival with all the cuts over his body. Kav'wai was holding his side, and his strength started to fail him. Azekiel sat Kav'wai down, supporting his back so Kav'wai could sit up straight, and then yelled for Airia himself.

Harmonus knelt next to his friend. "Kav'wai what happened?" he asked. "Did Ghamorrahk do this to you?"

Kav'wai nodded. "We didn't even sense him coming; the darkness jumped at us as hundreds of dresh'keer and dresh'kad swarmed us. Ghamorrahk put his spear through Mother right after she told me to run. I wanted to face him, but Sodomus attacked me. He was able to cut me a few times, but I got away, I had to let you know what happened." Airia finally got to Kav'wai and started entering her healing trance, only it was too late. She looked up at Harmonus with a sorrowful look and shook her head slightly. She then put her hand on Kav'wai's head and started to weep. Kav'wai looked up at Airia. "It's all right, Airia," he said. "I knew this would happen sooner or later; it was just a matter of time. Harmonus, when it's time, I need you to take my teva. Don't let them take it." Harmonus thought back on when his mother died and how similar it was to this moment. He couldn't even mumble a word; all he could do was nod.

Azekiel started to cry. "Leave us ... please." Azekiel wanted to be with his son during his last moments and say whatever needed to be said.

Harmonus walked up to Airia. "Get Korvinus. Sylvarus and some fifty sentials will go with you to the northern city. Build whatever vessel you can as fast as you can to get all of us across the endless sea."

Airia gave him a confused look. "Across? There are other lands beyond the waters?"

"I believe there are, but I can't be sure. Even if the darkness falls this very day, there won't be enough land to support the men. This war is between the aggelos; we can let an entire race die because of us.

I sent enough sentials with you to repopulate the land if necessary, so make sure you built something large enough to hold them. Then you can build more ships to hold the rest of the people." Airia nodded and started to leave when Harmonus called her name again. "We won't have much time. Azekiel will want revenge and will go on a rampage. The end of this war is near … do you understand?" Airia nodded and ran.

Harmonus knew all his uncle's wisdom would be gone now, replaced by a blind hatred that was fueled by rage. By now Ghamorrahk would have delivered news of his success to his master, Abbadon, and Abbadon was no fool. He'd know that Azekiel would retaliate; he would wait at the edge of the darkness with all the forces at his disposal, ready to kill the great warrior and take his mighty teva. The only way Azekiel would survive would be if Harmonus, Airandrius, and the rest of the Nivine army were with him. Harmonus just hoped that Abbadon wouldn't be ready for such a confrontation, though in his heart he knew Abbadon was.

Harmonus walked into the war room and saw a young lady cleaning the floors and chairs. As many times as he'd been in there, he'd never noticed all the people who took care of everything. He couldn't help but think how many innocent people died just so the rest could survive. How many loved ones died as the darkness swept through? It seemed an impossible task to count how many had died; it'd be like counting all the stars in the sky or all the grains of sand on the ground. All these people wanted was to live their lives in peace, and the aggelos, the most powerful race that ever walked this earth, couldn't even give them that. How much power would it take to save the ones you cared about or even to save yourself from the horrible acts of the world? How many more would have to die in this war, and how many more wars were yet to come? Harmonus thought back on Henvik, the first man to officially die in this war. Harmonus couldn't even count how many more had died, let alone remember them all. As he tried to think of all those who had died so that others could live, he was interrupted by Airandrius entering the room.

Airandrius walked over to his chair and sat down, flicking his wrist to dismiss the young lady. "What is it?" he said.

Harmonus shook his head. "I don't know how much longer we have, Father. Azekiel will no doubt enter the darkness to fight Abbadon, and Abbadon will be waiting for him along with his entire army."

Airandrius nodded. "We could try and calm him. He is the wisest of us; he of all people would see reason."

Harmonus shook his head again. "Would you see reason if you lost your children right after losing your wife?" Harmonus didn't wait to see Airandrius nod; he knew that he would. "I sent a little under fifty sentials to help Airia and Korvinus build something to get them over the waters. We could fly along with the harvos as—"

"I hope you aren't already thinking that we're going fail to save these lands."

"We've already failed, Father. Two cities a few hundred leagues apart is no kingdom; the men won't have enough resources to sustain themselves." Airandrius looked down at the map in front of him as he leaned back in his seat. "Mother told me that there were other lands, and the daimonion seem to believe there are other lands as well. This is our only hope."

"Harmonus ... aggelos and man were born from this land. To leave it wo—" Airandrius looked up to see Azekiel walking through the doorway carrying Kav'wai in his arms.

Harmonus could feel the teva leaving his friends body. He watched Azekiel place his son on the war table. Kav'wai was clenching his fists in pain; he looked at Harmonus and nodded. Azekiel walked out of the room and wept as Harmonus took what teva Kav'wai had left.

Azekiel sensed his son disappear. Airandrius walked over to his younger brother and sat down next to him. He then placed his hand on Azekiel's shoulder to try to comfort him. Harmonus walked over to sit and mourn with them in silence.

"Harmonus." Harmonus looked up to see Azekiel looking at him. "Teach me how to take teva."

Harmonus sat up straight. "Uncle, the only way to teach you would be to take the teva from the land."

"Then evacuate the city and keep the army in the northern city. Then we can face the darkness with everything we have left." Harmonus looked deep into his uncle's eyes, reading every thought and emotion that went through his mind. He was furious but still wise enough not to simply charge into the darkness. Harmonus nodded.

Chapter 10: A World Dies

With Varsol completely drained of all teva, Azekiel had finally learned how to siphon teva from another. Harmonus thought of teaching Airandrius as well but decided they didn't have enough time or enough teva in the land to do so.

"Just remember, Uncle," Harmonus said, "you'll have to weaken Ghamorrahk to be able to siphon the teva from him. They learned just as you two did how to stop me from naturally taking your teva when I was young." Azekiel nodded. It only took some twelve moons to learn, but in those twelve moons, Azekiel had hardly said a word. He didn't care about anything else anymore; he just wanted his blade to taste Ghamorrahk's blood. Harmonus had to keep a watchful eye on his uncle to make sure his hair hadn't changed. He hated the fact that he couldn't trust his uncle anymore, but teva can corrupt so easily.

Harmonus looked up at the sky and closed his eyes to feel the sun's beautiful light—yet another thing so many take for granted until it's nearly taken from them. The darkness started to advance slowly. Harmonus had known it would sooner or later, and without any teva in the land, there was no reason for them to stay there. Now the only city left alive was Kendel. Most of its residents fished on the seashore or built small vessels that allowed one or two men to fish in deeper waters. Like all the other cities, it hadn't had any walls until the war started and forced them to build walls that left all the farmland outside and kept everything else inside. Kendel was not by any means a well-fortified or tactically placed city. The only natural defense it had was the bay on the east side of the city; as far as they knew, dresh'kad couldn't swim. Harmonus knew the city wouldn't last long once the darkness arrived. Their fate would be decided outside the walls of the last Nivinian city.

The army led by Harmonus's sentials was in formation outside the city walls. When Harmonus approached the army, Sylvarus walked up to greet him and the other two aggelos and brought his fist to his chest. "Your army is ready, Hegemon."

Harmonus looked at the men standing before him. They stared at the advancing darkness without flinching, but looks are deceiving. Harmonus could feel the fear in their hearts. They knew they faced obliteration, but what else could they do? This war wasn't about land or power for them; it was about the right to survive. Each and every one of them knew they were going to die, and they feared it. Yet they dared not show it. The heart of men was a very strange and interesting thing to observe. Harmonus wanted to reassure them that all would be well and that victory was at hand, but he couldn't bring himself to lie to them. Even if they survived this war, it would be no victory for any of them.

"My lord"—Sylvarus was looking over Harmonus's shoulder—"the darkness approaches. What are our orders?"

Harmonus looked over his right shoulder to see the light fading away. He looked back at Sylvarus, his greatest companion amongst man, and felt the fear in his heart. But as he looked at his friend, he sensed peace. He knew he was going to die and that the teva that kept him alive would be drained, and yet he was at peace. Sylvarus was proud to die alongside his mentor; his loyalty was beyond what Harmonus had ever shown anyone else himself. There was a lesson, it seemed, to be learned from the young race of man.

"How many are at the bay, Sylvarus?" Harmonus asked.

"Forty-six sentials are helping Airia and Korvinus, Hegemon. The rest are out here."

"I need you to be the forty-seventh. If I am unsuccessful, I need you to be hegemon to Korvinus. Make sure they escape the darkness; this is my last and most important charge for you."

Sylvarus reached his arm out, a gesture that signified the greeting of brothers that was frowned upon between races. Harmonus didn't care; Sylvarus was loyal to the very end, and he wanted to make sure Sylvarus knew that he appreciated it. He grasped Sylvarus's forearm and put his left hand on the man's shoulder. Sylvarus mirrored his master. They nodded, and Sylvarus left for the bay, knowing he would never see his master again.

Harmonus looked at the men that stood before him yet again. He wanted to talk to them, to make some encouraging speech that may motivate them, but it wouldn't matter. No matter what he said, no one would remember it once the darkness reached them. He turned around to face the darkness with Airandrius and Azekiel by his side and felt a massive wind from the north. Harmonus smiled. It was time to see what his harvos could do against the beasts in the dark. Abrox landed to the right of Harmonus, and the other two harvos landed right next to Abrox. All of them were ready for the battle, or as ready as they would ever be, at least. Abrox stood like a colossus next to his master. His deep breaths echoed through the empty land.

As the darkness drew closer the silence stopped, replaced by what sounded like thousands of dresh'kad charging forward to devour their prey. Harmonus didn't need to hear them to know they were at the edge of the darkness; he could sense thousands of both dresh'kad and dresh'keer in the darkness. He didn't need to see the wave of darkness rushing forward to know the three remaining daimonion led the assault. The darkness was a few leagues away now and coming fast, like a river that just broke through a dam. Harmonus summoned his staff and held it out parallel to the ground, creating a blue light that acted as a shield to the city. Harmonus wouldn't be able to hold the shield once he was attacked, but it would stop the momentum of the initial rush.

Airandrius and Azekiel drew their blades as the darkness slammed into Harmonus's shield of light. The harvos let out a roar that shook the earth, motivating the men to let out a cry of war that seemed like it could echo through time. Abbadon, Ghamorrahk, and Sodomus jumped through the light barrier and charged forward at Harmonus. They knew that if they could at least distract Harmonus, the cursed wall of light would come down and their army of the dark could continue. Azekiel went straight for Ghamorrahk as Airandrius went for Abbadon. Harmonus thought for sure that Sodomus would come for him, but he instead went to aid Abbadon against Airandrius. They must have felt the power difference in Airandrius and decided to kill the aggelos one at a time so that they could then gang up on Harmonus. Sodomus leapt high in the air, bringing his hammer above his head to smash down on the distracted Airandrius. Harmonus wanted to yell for his father but knew it would only distract him further.

At the last moment, Abrox whipped his tail into Sodomus, slamming him hard into the ground. Abrox charged down in an attempt to get his prey, but he was too slow. Sodomus jumped out of the way only to have his leg caught in the teeth of Ilsox. Sodomus held his large hammer by the end of its hilt and swung it into the side of Ilsox's muzzle. Ilsox roared in pain, releasing Sodomus, but Sodomus didn't have a break, for Ibrex and Abrox were on him in a flash. Ilsox rejoined them within seconds. Harmonus's beasts were powerful, but they couldn't possibly bring down a daimonion. They were just buying their master some time.

Harmonus could feel the darkness continuing to smash into his barrier from nearly all sides but the one bounded by the sea. He looked at the fight between the ones he loved most and the ones he hated. He wanted to help but knew that once he lowered the light, the darkness would rush in and make things even more difficult. He would have to wait until he was absolutely needed, no matter how much he didn't want to. He looked over at Azekiel. Ghamorrahk was more powerful than Azekiel, but Azekiel fought with an unrelenting rage. He seemed to take no care for himself; he just wanted to bash his opponent's defense with no regard for his own. Harmonus had never seen such ferocity in his uncle before, but it may just have been what they need to win this fateful battle.

Airandrius knew he wouldn't last long against Abbadon, not when Abbadon had so much teva running through him and Airandrius had so little. He was on the defensive, giving ground each time Abbadon brought his blade down on Airandrius. He didn't dare call out for help; Harmonus would no doubt come, but then the darkness would too. Then their army would be slaughtered. He had to give Airia and Korvinus the time they needed to finish their vessel to cross the great waters; he wouldn't accept death until he knew his children were safe. It was hard enough to think that his oldest wouldn't survive, but he would rather die side by side with his greatest son than anything else.

Harmonus kept watching the battle. Airandrius was struggling, but Azekiel was battering down his opponent. Either Azekiel would beat his opponent down to the point that he couldn't defend himself or Ghamorrahk would get Azekiel when he left an opening. With Azekiel being purely on the offensive, it seemed either had an equal chance of happening. Then just as Harmonus thought of it, Azekiel left himself open on his left side. Ghamorrahk saw the opening and drove his spear into Azekiel's ribs. Harmonus was about to lower the shield when he noticed Azekiel grab Ghamorrahk's spear and drive it in further. He then sliced his blade through Ghamorrahk's neck, severing his head completely. Azekiel left himself open on purpose to get a clear shot at Ghamorrahk. He had had his revenge, but he was terribly wounded.

At that same moment, Abbadon cut Airandrius's thigh and then sliced his chest, forcing Airandrius to the ground. He was about to finish Airandrius off when he felt Azekiel try to siphon Ghamorrahk's teva in an attempt to heal himself. Abbadon barked an order to Sodomus and then started sprinting toward the weakened aggelos. Abbadon knew Azekiel would be too powerful to stop if he took all the teva Ghamorrahk had gathered; he would simply kill Azekiel while he was weak and take the teva from both of them. He would allow Sodomus to kill Airandrius.

Harmonus had a split second to react, yet in that split second, it felt like time had slowed to a standstill. He thought of every memory he had of his beloved uncle, the one he cared most about. He knew he couldn't save him. Azekiel would gladly have given his life just for the possibility that his older brother would live. Harmonus knew exactly what Azekiel wanted him to do, but he couldn't. Abbadon's blade was about to pierce Azekiel's back and go through his heart, and Sodomus had his hammer in full swing, ready to smash the head of the lord of aggelos. Harmonus knew he couldn't save both of them. He knew the moment this battle started that this would happen, but he couldn't accept it.

Harmonus closed his eyes and charged forward with his staff out in front of him. In a flash of light, he cut Sodomus's arm off and then brought his staff up through his chest into his head. He drained the daimonion of his teva before he could even scream, lowering his staff as the daimonion disappeared. Harmonus turned to see Abbadon's blade plunged through his uncle. Shock was the first thing Harmonus recognized in his uncle's face. Then as Azekiel turned toward his nephew,

Harmonus saw peace in his eyes, and he disappeared. Harmonus was filled with hatred; it was the first time he had felt such a burning passion that no other word could describe.

Harmonus roared as he charged at Abbadon. He was ready to end this once and for all. Right before he reached Abbadon, the darkness swept in, and thousands of dresh'kad were upon them. He slaughtered dozens at a time only to have more take their place. For a moment he was worried that Abbadon would go after Airandrius, but then he felt his harvos guarding the wounded aggelos. The harvos would be able to hold back Abbadon until Harmonus arrived, which meant that Abbadon wouldn't even bother to attack them until Harmonus himself was dealt with.

Harmonus could hear the men of his army, both sential and army guard alike, scream as dresh'kad claws ripped through their armor. The sentials could take on a couple of dresh'kad, but they stood no chance against the winged dresh'keer. He wanted to help them, but he knew Abbadon's army was as large as the sea. The only way to stop them was to kill their leader. Harmonus could feel Abbadon trying to control his power behind a legion of dresh'keer. He thought Harmonus wouldn't be foolish enough to attack that many at once, but he was wrong. Harmonus charged straight into them, charging his staff with so much teva that even the dresh'keer tried to steer clear it. It took only a few moments to break through the dresh'keer and confront Abbadon.

"You've lost, Harmonus. Your land is destroyed, and your family will be consumed by the darkness. You've lost all cause to fight. Tell me what hope you have left, oh Father of Hope."

Harmonus didn't answer. He had nothing to say to the abomination, he just wanted to kill him. He shot out his left hand and let the thunderous light leap from his palm toward his target. Then he slammed his fist into the ground, causing the earth to shoot up spikes from underneath

Abbadon in an attempt to impale him. Abbadon expected the light and dodged it easily, but he was only on one foot when the ground drove up spikes at him. He was forced to jump. Abbadon barely had enough time to block Harmonus's staff in mid-air; he hadn't thought that Harmonus was that powerful, but Harmonus still wasn't powerful enough. Abbadon backflipped off the shockwave caused by their zeyaks smashing together. He landed quickly and shot back up at Harmonus. Harmonus's speed didn't seem to count for much against Abbadon; he was too powerful to attack recklessly. Every attack he made was countered, and every counter he made was dodged. Moreover, every moment they weren't clashing, a group of dresh'kad or dresh'keer attacked.

Harmonus shot light, fire, and earth at his opponent, and yet Abbadon still kept up his relentless assault. Each time Harmonus got some space, Abbadon would charge in to close it. He knew Harmonus couldn't defend himself as well up close. Abbadon seemed to know every move Harmonus could make with his staff, making his assaults nearly useless. Harmonus thought back on Azekiel's teachings. "Once I know how you fight, the fights over," Azekiel had said. Abbadon had not only taken Azekiel's power but had taken his combat knowledge as well. Harmonus had to think of something fast before Abbadon found an opening and exploited it.

Harmonus tried turning invisible, but Abbadon could sense him too easily. So he made his staff invisible, making Abbadon guess where to block and putting him on the defensive. Yet even that wasn't enough. Harmonus tried to stab Abbadon and missed. Abbadon used the opening to bring his blade down on Harmonus's head. Harmonus tried to back out of the way but was too late. Abbadon's blade sliced through the right side of Harmonus's face. Harmonus slammed his staff into the ground, creating a shockwave that sent Abbadon reeling backward.

Harmonus wanted to pursue, but he couldn't even see out of his right eye. He could feel the poison from the blade entering his skull.

The pain didn't have the effect Abbadon wanted. Instead of causing Harmonus to shriek in pain, it just threw Harmonus into a rage. He placed his hand on the wound for just a moment and then charged Abbadon, spinning his staff in a wild *X* pattern. Abbadon finally pinned Harmonus's staff to the ground only to be head-butted by the enraged aggelos. Abbadon backed off. Then he reached out and grabbed Harmonus's staff. Harmonus realized how powerful Abbadon must have been to be able to do that without being incinerated. Harmonus let go of his staff, causing it to disappear, and brought his fist into Abbadon's chin. Before the daimonion could regain balance, Harmonus grabbed him by the throat and shot into the air, breathing in deeply as thy ascended. Once they broke through the darkness, Harmonus threw his enemy into the air and let out his breath as a bright, blue flame that engulfed Abbadon. Once Harmonus was out of breath, he summoned his staff and flew above Abbadon in a flash. He drove his staff through Abbadon's back as they plunged back down into the darkness.

They hit the earth with a force that created a small crater. Harmonus thrust his staff completely through Abbadon, creating a large crevice in the ground that went on for leagues. Abbadon screamed as Harmonus charged his staff more and more, trying to tear Abbadon to shreds from the inside out. Before Harmonus could finish the job, Abbadon summoned his sword and slashed Harmonus's calf, causing him to scream and drop to his knee in pain. Harmonus let go of his staff, and it disappeared. Abbadon took that opportunity to roll over and bring his sword into Harmonus's lower stomach.

Harmonus leaned forward in shock. He knew it was over. He could feel Abbadon's blade siphon the teva out of him. He felt the darkness start to take over, willing him to give up. He could feel the life-force of

Abbadon through his zeyak. Even his teva wanted to flee him and go toward the light. Then Harmonus realized how Abbadon did it; he used his blade a conductor to connect his teva with that of others. Harmonus grabbed the blade and thrust it deeper, looking into Abbadon's confused eyes. Realization dawned in Abbadon's eyes as he felt his own teva leave him. Harmonus didn't need to learn how to siphon teva; it was his gift, just like his command over light. When Abbadon tried to take Harmonus's teva, it gave Harmonus a direct link to Abbadon's teva. Harmonus hardly had to focus to allow the teva to flow into him. Abbadon flinched in pain as the teva continued to leave him. He tried to remove his blade or even let go of it, but it was useless. He was far too weak already. Abbadon screamed as the last of his teva drained out of him, causing his body to disappear abruptly.

The power flowed through Harmonus in a rush, but it was too late for him. The darkness wasn't leaving his body. Harmonus knew he had to get rid of the darkness in order to kill off the dresh'kad before he left this world. He lifted his staff above his head, draining all of his teva into it. At first fear stayed his hand, but then he could see his mother tending her gardens and Henvik with his family. He thought back on Azekiel laughing with his family and all the other aggelos living in peace before the war. He thought of his younger siblings and father; they would live and ensure the survival of this fragile world. The hope of their future quelled his fear; his sacrifice would be enough for the world to live in peace.

Harmonus slammed his staff into the ground, creating a wave of energy that rivaled that of the sun. It swept across the land, disintegrating all the dark ones in its path and lifting the darkness. Ilsox and Ibrex fanned out their wings to protect Airia and the others by the ship, and Abrox held Airandrius close to his chest with his wings covering him. The light reflected harmlessly off the harvos' crystal-like scales, protecting all that stood behind them while all else became rubble.

Airandrius came out from under Abrox. He looked at the destroyed earth that was before him. Realizing what must have happened, he searched and yelled for his son. Airia and Korvinus ran up to congratulate them on their victory only to see Airandrius searching under rubble for Harmonus. Airandrius started to become frantic. He wasn't sure where Harmonus and Abbadon had battled through the darkness, and he couldn't feel Harmonus's teva. The harvos flew up into the air, searching the land for their master.

Abrox spotted Harmonus and roared as he landed next to him to let the others know that he had found him. Airandrius and the others ran at the sound only to see Harmonus lying with his face in the ground.

"No!" Airandrius fell to his knees at the sight of his lifeless son.

Airia ran past him and lifted Harmonus's head in desperation. Tears started coming down her cheek. "He can't be gone. He can't. His body is still here, so he's still ... still alive ..."

Korvinus walked up next to Airia. "Then why can't we feel his teva?"

Airia didn't answer.

Chapter 11: A New World

Harmonus felt sand underneath him and heard waves rolling onto the beach. At first he thought he was in Kendel but soon concluded he wasn't. There was teva in the land here—a lot of teva—and it seemed to stretch as far as Harmonus reached out. He opened his eyes to see the blue sky above him, a deep, beautiful blue that he hadn't seen in what seemed like an eternity. He sat up to see a calm sea and a beach that wrapped around a cliff that was nearly a hundred leagues high. The ground quaked as Abrox landed beside him, and Harmonus laughed as Abrox smothered him in his excitement.

"Harmonus! Father, Korvinus, come quickly. He's awake!" Harmonus barely had enough time to turn his head to see Airia embrace him with tears in her eyes. "We thought you were gone, Brother!" Korvinus and Airandrius ran around the corner as fast as they could to embrace him.

After they got their fill of hugs, Airandrius stepped back and put his arm on Harmonus shoulder. "We couldn't feel your teva. I thought you were dead! Now it feels as if your teva is stronger than the very sun."

Harmonus nodded. "I must have subconsciously blocked off my teva so I wouldn't harm anyone." Harmonus looked around. "Where are we?"

Airandrius pointed at the sea. "We're across the endless sea. You were right; there were other lands out here, and they're flowing with teva."

Harmonus looked out at the sea. "How long did it take to cross the waters?"

"Well, your harvos were able to get here in about nine moons, give or take one or two, but the water vessels took nearly three seasons."

Harmonus thought about how fast his harvos could fly, trying to calculate how far they were. "How long was I asleep?"

Airia stepped forward. "You started to twitch after the first moon, but you've been asleep almost a year. We were beginning to wonder if you would ever wake."

Harmonus couldn't believe he had been asleep for that long. Then he saw Sylvarus running toward him. "Hegemon! I'm glad to see you're finally awake and in good health."

Harmonus smiled. "How many made it?"

Sylvarus's joyful look was replaced with one of sorrow. "Only those you assigned to me, Hegemon. If any did survive the battle, they died when you let off that wave of energy. We would have died as well if not for your harvos."

Harmonus looked around. "Speaking of which, where are Ibrex and Ilsox?"

Airia cleared her throat. "I asked them to go back to Nivine and see if there was any darkness left in the land. I hope you don't mind. I'm surprised they were even willing to listen to me."

Harmonus nodded then walked with Airandrius on a pathway up the cliff. When they reached the top, Harmonus saw what he suspected was the baseline of a new city. Harmonus looked up at his father. "Care if I go take a look at the land?"

Airandrius smiled and looked up at Abrox, who wouldn't go more than a few meters away from Harmonus. "Of course. That is, if your faithful companion doesn't mind."

Harmonus smiled and walked up to Abrox. "Care to give me a lift?" Abrox made a playful grunt and brought his neck down to allow his master to climb on. Then Abrox launched into the air and shot across the sky. Harmonus noticed that they had landed on a series of very large isles that were next to another stretch of land that went as far as he could see. Harmonus closed his eyes and felt the wind fly by, thinking of all that had transpired. Though the sacrifice was high, they had survived, and even though he wouldn't consider it a victory, it was enough. When all else had failed and the darkness circled around them, hope had remained. That was all they needed. Now it was time to rebuild and ensure that the corruption had been purged from the land. Now was the time for peace.

Made in the USA
Monee, IL
15 March 2021